THE TIDAL DETECTIVE SERIES: BOARDWALKS AND FLIPFLOPS

A Kiawah Island Mystery

Vanna Byrd

*Created for Carol and BB
beautiful life long friends,
cohorts in beach mischief.*

*Dedicated to Casey
husband, best friend
better half and partner in life.*

*Special Thank you:
Madison, Diana, Terri, Leigh,
Jennifer, Kristina, Karla, Marian
and Charles for encouraging
me along the way. Without each
of you, the story would
remain unfinished!*

CONTENTS

Title Page
Dedication

Chapter 1	1
Chapter 2	22
Chapter 3	25
Chapter 4	26
Chapter 5	29
Chapter 6	42
Chapter 7	45
Chapter 8	52
Chapter 9	56
Chapter 10	58
Chapter 11	63
Chapter 12	66
Chapter 13	69
Chapter 14	71
Chapter 15	74

Chapter 16	76
Chapter 17	81
Chapter 18	86
Chapter 19	88
Chapter 20	92
Chapter 21	100
Chapter 22	108
Chapter 23	113
Chapter 24	114
Chapter 25	117
Chapter 26	122
Chapter 27	126
Chapter 28	134
Chapter 29	140
Chapter 30	145
Chapter 31	149
Chapter 32	159
Want more?	163
About The Author	165

CHAPTER 1

CU@PA#16N12

Friday, April 14

Officer Brooke Mason answered her phone at 6:24am:

"Joleen, What the heck? Why are you calling so early? I'm barley awake...on my first cup of coffee."

Joleen's Tennessee accent, which was a Dolly Parton-like Southern drawl with twang began:

"Listen Honey, a fella was walking his dog on the beach at Kiawah this mornin and found a dead body...over near PA16. You know Palmer's on leave. Looks like this one's yours."

"Suicide or an accidental overdose?" Immediately, Brooke was wide awake.

"Nope, suspicious death. It'd be your first lead investigation... if you get your behind over there."

"On my way now! And Joleen, maybe, If I do a great job on this one, I'll finally be promoted to the unit. Thanks for the heads up! I owe you one!"

She began to think about how she would need to organize the forensic investigation.

I want to assign each detective to fully use their strengths...

First to come to mind was Officer Benedict. He was already a part of the homicide unit and had more job experience. He excelled at the art of intimidation. Brooke had witnessed his effective use to gain control of chaotic scenes. But he was not the greatest at deductive reasoning. She questioned his ability to take directions from someone with less experience. The current Head Investigator for the Homicide Unit, Bob Palmer, had appointed Brooke instead of Benedict to be his replacement during his medical absence. Many had questioned his decision. However, she planned to use this opportunity to break out of the pack of detectives in Charleston County.

Now is my time to shine. Don't screw this up.

Brooke received Joleen's message and loaded the address at PA 16. Looking at the screen, she noted that the ride from the turnabout to the victim would take 12 minutes.

Of course! At the far end of the island.

Kiawah is a barrier island, parallel to the mainland and surrounded by water. It is a skinny island with only one bridge entrance for auto or bike traffic. Everything exclusive is at the other end of the island.

Twelve minutes until my dream job begins. Don't screw this up.

Since she was 17 years old, Brooke had dreamed of becoming a lead investigator. She had reminded herself of her goal every night before falling asleep.

When I'm a detective on a homicide unit, I'll follow the facts, not the politics.

She really didn't want to be involved in the politics of police work. The bad publicity during recent years to "defund" the police had heavily influenced her decision to become an officer. Her pursuit of the truth was noble, unwavering, and yet naive. She was not one to be influenced by other people or pressured by her peers. When problem solving, her brain would not rest, exploring several possibilities and theories concurrently. She would explore each aspect of a clue to the fullest extent. It was her compulsion.

Now driving, she began to reflect on the difficulty she had in school. A nontraditional learner; questioning everything that was taught from a very early age, Brooke had made poor impressions on her teacher every year: In first grade, when she refused to taste "stone soup"; In second grade, when she demanded her right to "freely move about the room." In third grade, it was the broken window.

On the second day of third grade, she kicked the ground during recess. Unfortunately, the kicked-up dirt contained a sharp rock which hit the glass pane of the school cafeteria window at just the correct angle to completely shatter the highly visible window into hundreds of tiny pieces. Shocked at the result, Brooke found it hard to believe that it had happened. Immediately, she was escorted to the office of the vice-principal. Again, Brooke did not make a good impression. She felt defeated in her ability to develop a relationship with an authority figure.

Luckily in high school, Brooke had another "fresh start": attending a new school with a forensic science teacher, who not only helped her hone her deductive skills, but she was also an inspiration and role model. Mrs. Westwood was a great mentor who helped Brooke to realize her potential. More importantly, gave her an ember of self-confidence and showed her the value of her own curiosity. Mrs. Westwood had taken an interest in Brooke, explaining to her that not everyone has this superpower, and even if they did have a knack for deduction and problem solving, they may not have the emotional stamina required to pursue the truth.

Thank you, Mrs. Westwood. I hope to do you proud!

Returning her thoughts to the task at hand, she neared her destination. She made the right turn into the parking area at Mariner's Watch. Part of the Kiawah Island Resort, Mariner's Watch is a small group of Villas between the beach and bike path. Brooke was relieved that a patrol officer had closed the parking lot and was scanning IDs.

Great, at least they already have the parking

area secure.

She pulled up to the officer and instantly recognized his round silhouette as John Dawkins; A shorter fella with an extremely large, round belly, dark, almost black slicked-back shiny hair, and short arms in relation to his body. Familiar with his macho attitude after working together for the last seven years, Brooke wondered if Dawkins knew he was not her favorite patrol officer. Or if he cared that his career was stagnant, stuck scanning IDs.

"Hey Brooke, What the hell are you doing here? Where's Palmer."

"Thanks for your concern about my schedule, Dawkins. This one's mine."

"Sure...! You're kidding, right?"

Brooke was not in the mood to deal with macho man John, although she often kept a running count as she talked with him, just to see how long he'd be able to suck in his gut. She had noticed the behavior shortly after meeting him, that he held his elbows away from his body, and flexed his fat covered pectoral muscles each time someone approached him. Usually, she would extend the conversation on purpose to see just how long he could hold the "Hans and Franz" pose without taking a deep breath. Sometimes she may even giggle, while controlling the impulse to clap to the "Hear me now and believe this later." phrase from the decades old SNL skit.

Not today. I'm a woman on a mission. Need

to focus on the investigation. Just be the decision maker based on facts. First, gather and organize information about the scene.

"Scan every ID that enters and exits the area, collect all of the license plate numbers in the parking lot, and send it to Joleen."

"Where is Palmer? Who put you in charge?" He was still holding his Hans and Franz pose.

Annoyed with Dawkins questioning her authority, Brooke didn't answer. Instead, she pulled forward, parked her car and walked to the bike path leading to the beach.

Brooke called Joleen:

"Joleen, what do you have?"

She was all business:

"Called in at 6:17am by Wayne Shealy, he's on scene with Detective Benedict. Detective Corey's securing the scene, Detectives Howard and Daniel are en route."

"Great! Tell Benedict to keep him on scene. I'll question him after I give the team assignments. Joleen, Patrolman John Dawkins will be scanning vehicle tags and IDs in the area. Let me know when the data has all been uploaded."

Brooke ended the call and walked following the coordinates. They led Brooke to the beach #16 public access boardwalk, called PA16 by the locals. She arrived at the parking area at 6:46 am and walked down the bike trail, to the top of the boardwalk and just over the dune. Reaching the beach just as the sunrise broke out over the ocean horizon, she tilted her head back with her eyes closed to feel the warmth of the sunrise against her face. This was the ritual she performed nearly every morning during her jog before starting her day. Over the last seven years of running on the beach, Brooke had lost her muffin top and developed a flat belly, toning her petite but solid body. She had grown to love her morning self-pep-talk on the beach. However, this morning was different, instead she needed to use leadership to organize the scene on the beach. The pause only lasted a second as she gathered her thoughts.

Brooke performed a quick internet search:
Sunrise at 6:47 am.
Sunset at 7:53 pm.
High tides at 8:23 am and 8:43 pm.
Low tide at 2:19 pm.

Soon, the shore would be busy with vacationers eager to catch their glimpse of the sunrise and collect the newly revealed shells.

Brooke began to prioritize and triage team assignments based on the tides and coworker strengths.

High tides decrease the width of the beach, forcing beach walkers closer to the dunes. The rising tide would also erase important clues, washing away footprints, fingerprints, fibers, and DNA evidence. With the tide rising to its peak at 8:23 am this morning, it only gave the homicide unit an hour and 33 minutes to collect any evidence on the beach, assuming the scene hadn't already been contaminated by the early morning beachcombers.

Using her hand radio to take command of the scene:

"Rope the scene all the way to the tide line. No owner or guest will pass the PA16 until we search every inch of beach. Divert any cyclists to remain on the bike path and keep the beachgoers back at public access #15".

Brooke immediately approached one of her favorite coworkers, Detective Corley, who had already used yellow crime scene tape to secure the boardwalk and stairs around the body.

Corley and Brooke had graduated from the police academy together 8 years ago and both had a knack for detective work. However, the short guy with light blonde, wavy hair and a passion for photography had become one of the best crime scene videographers in the unit. As she approached, he didn't stop unpacking his gear but glanced up to Brooke:

"What do you know?"

"Only been on the scene for four or five minutes. I didn't get up close and personal. Roped it off before I got a good look."

Pointing under the boardwalk and nodding his head toward the dunes, Corley continued.

"It's a blue beach towel buried under the boardwalk with foot and ankle exposed. I'm getting my equipment set up now to photograph the scene."

Corley was pulling lights, battery packs,

and camera lenses out of a large aluminum case. Not wanting to wait for him to set up the lights before she assessed the scene, Brooke impatiently opened his equipment bag. Then donned gloves, a hair net, and shoe covers before approaching the boardwalk. She looked under the wooden steps stretching towards the dune. Brooke could see the frayed edges of a blue beach towel peeking through the sand. Then, dots of bright blue reflected back as she shone her flashlight into the darkness. Brooke stepped to the side of the boardwalk and squatted down for a better look. From this angle, she saw part of an ankle, left foot, and toes with blue nail polish exposed from the sand. Using her gloved hand, she checked for a pedal pulse by placing three fingers over the top of the foot. Not only was there no pulse, but the foot was pale and cold to touch.

"Corley, listen. We don't know if it's a full body, a mutilated body, or just part of a body. We do know that there is no pulse and that the foot is cold to touch."

Standing up to face the crime scene photographer, she turned, then suddenly froze. A dark smudge on the wooden post caught her eye. She used her flashlight to get a better look. The smudge was in the shape of a handprint.

A handprint? Definitely looks like blood.

"Corley, first go to the shore and capture a video of the sand before the tide washes any evidence away. Use a grid pattern to record a video of every inch of the beach. Then, come back and get stills of this handprint and the area around the victim."

Brooke pulled up her recent contacts, selected Joleen and spoke

"ETA of our M.E. to PA16?" There was a pause. Then Joleen's southern drawl came across the police radio:

"Coroner Burgess, ETA 12 minutes, entering the turnabout now."

Meanwhile, our crime scene is being washed away.

She responded to Joleen again:

"Detective Unit ETA?"

"Detectives Daniels and Howard are arriving on scene now."

Brooke turned and walked quickly to the parking area. She intercepted Matt Daniels and Robert Howard as they stepped out of the white crime unit van and opened the sliding door. Daniels, known for pulling his weight on the team, had been on the unit for over 15 years and was well liked by other detectives. Although he had his back towards her, she recognized his wide shoulders and long, rectangular torso. The slightly balding fellow, Daniels, turned revealing his glasses and spoke first,

"Joleen gave us the scoop. We have a suspicious death on the island the day after Palmer, our lead investigator, goes on medical leave and he requests that you be made lead investigator instead of Detective Benedict. Can you believe that?"

Happy to hear Daniels's straight-to-the-point version of the story, she broke into a wide grin and pressed them for action.

"Start at the shoreline, at the water. The tide is rising, and we're losing our crime scene. High tide is 8:23. Corley's gathering video evidence in a grid pattern. As soon as he finishes an area, you start to gather physical evidence. Then, remove the sand from around the victim. The coroner will be here shortly and be anxious to remove the body. Don't let him do that until we have collected our evidence. There's smudge on the wood boardwalk post. After Corely gets'the stills, collect samples, could be blood."

Having remained silent since their arrival, Detective Howard, much taller and slimmer than Detective Daniels agreed first.

"We're on it. We've got your back on this."

"Thanks Robert, I appreciate it."

Relieved for his support, she turned and walked back towards PA 16. Corley, finishing up with the beach sand video, began to set up lighting for his next video assignment, the sand around the boardwalk and the dunes. When he was approached by another officer. Wearing his mirror sunglasses, Detective Benedict, a monolithic, 6'-6", muscular handsome man, approached the boardwalk:

"Corley, Have you seen Palmer? I'm having a

hard time keeping the 911 caller on the scene. Says that he's got to get to a conference meeting."

Hearing a familiar voice, Brooke turned to see Benedict and Corley as they stood beside each other looking like Schwarenegger and DeVito in Twins, Benedict standing at least a foot taller than his coworker with a stern face, dark hair, muscular wide shoulders and an almost foreboding appearance. While Corley, a blonde, short stature, fit guy with friendly facial expressions, looked much more approachable. Brooke interjected:

"I'm lead on this one. Where is the caller?" Brooke turned to Benedict;

"Run his license, get an address and a background check, then let me know what you find."

She made her way down the beach to the 911 caller. Once Brooke approached the caller's beach chair. She knelt down on one knee to be able to better see his face. She needed to read his facial expressions and body language.

"Mr. Shealy. I'm the lead investigator, Detective Brooke Mason. I need to ask you a few more questions before we release you from the scene."

Brooke held her badge out towards the distraught man. He sat in a beach chair, holding his head in his hands with his dog's leash around his wrist. Wayne Shealy warily looked up, obviously anxious, and with trembling hands, reached to shake Brooke's while still sitting. On an average day, he may have been handsome. However, today his light brown weary eyes were red and full of horror and dismay. Wayne's dark blonde curly hair was wildly frizzy blowing in the beach wind. His big golden yellow dog was sitting loyally at his feet with his chin resting on his owner's thigh as if trying to comfort the man.

"Mr. Shealy, please, Start from the beginning. What time did you wake up this morning?"

"about 5:15. Tyler woke me up."

"Who is Tyler?"

"This is Tyler," petting the golden retriever on his head with both hands. Tyler's ears perked up and his tail started wagging slowly as he recognized his name.

"Ok so Tyler wakes you up at 5:15 this morning."

"Yeah, he was insistent that I take him outside. As a matter of fact, he was restless last night and woke me up many times whimpering and pacing. You know, being in a new place and all, neither one of us really slept well."

Lead investigator Brooke Mason interrupted: "What did you do at 5:15 when your dog woke you?"

"Well to be honest, I threw on my PJ bottoms and took Tyler quickly outside to pee. We came down the wooden stairs of the Villa and he peed on the big pine tree out back. He wanted to go to the beach but I wouldn't go. Then we came back inside. I made coffee, fed him, went to the bathroom, threw on my shorts, and came out to the beach to watch the sunrise."

Brooke pressed for a timeline. "What time did you come out onto the beach this morning?"

"It was just a minute or two before 6 am. I remember because I had to silence my alarm while I was setting up my beach chair."

"Did you see anyone on the beach?"

"No, it was still dark."

"Ok, go ahead. You got to the beach just before 6:00. Set up your chair. Then what?"

"We started to play fetch on the beach with a frisbee. But Tyler kept running to the boardwalk and barking."

After following his excessively barking golden retriever to the edge of the dunes, Wayne looked under the boardwalk with his phone flashlight, expecting to see the remains of a horseshoe crab or a strayed blue crab. He noticed a flash of blue color and got closer to investigate. The color turned out to be toes with bright blue toenail polish. Tyler had begun to dig up the foot and continued to bark incessantly while continuing to sniff and dig at the sand. Wayne grabbed Tyler's leash to pull him away and called 911.

"Can I leave now? It's 7:32? Got to git Tyler settled, pull it together, and git to the conference."

"Yes, thank you Mr Shealy, after you give Detective Benedict your contact info you can leave.

We may have more questions for you later."

Brooke waved to Benedict to come over. "Detective Benedict, Would you please walk Mr. Shealy to his villa? Get his car tag and contact info to Joleen in case we have more questions later."

"Yes, Ma'am." In a southern drawl: "You heard her, once we git to the condo, you put that dog away. Then, hand over your driver's license and auto registration." Mr. Shealy, his dog and Benedict disappeared down the beach toward the bike path, then out of sight, towards the villas.

Brooke headed back to the boardwalk at public access #16. The beach was now well lit as the sun continued to rise in the morning sky. A few beach walkers were standing outside the yellow taped off area, in dismay that part of the beach was blocked without any explanation. She approached the investigation scene thinking how well Benedict had just reacted to her being the lead investigator.

He didn't even skip a beat, just carried out the orders as soon as I asked. Unexpectedly, Benedict didn't question a thing. With all of his experience, I thought he'd be a real dict about it.

As Brooke returned to PA16, Corley was now under the side of the boardwalk taking photos of the exposed foot. She squatted down beside him and looked under the boardwalk. Seeing the victim under the photography lighting, Brooke was able to see a blue beach towel peeking out from under the mound of sand. Its edges were tucked in around a mound and sealed with sand. One corner of the towel was uncovered and revealed a small pasty colored ankle and foot. From behind her, Brooke heard someone call her name:

"Detective Mason!"

Startled, she turned to recognize the tall thin older gentleman with short white hair. It was Coroner Burgess, who was approaching from the parking area. Brooke knew that she needed to keep the scene contamination-free for a little longer. Having worked side by side with him at auto accidents along Bohicket Road, she knew that he was always in a hurry to take charge of a body. When arriving on the scene, "Newman" always popped into Brooke's head. She appreciated his intelligence. However, he had a knack for pushing people's buttons on purpose.

Speaking quickly, Coroner Burgess started to don gloves, hair net and shoe coverings.

"Joleen told me that you are the lead. What do we have?"

"Called in this morning at 6:17am. Found by a beach walker and his dog, under the boardwalk. There's all or part of a victim wrapped in a towel and covered with sand. So far, we can see an exposed ankle and foot. Not sure of the condition of the body. Corley is finishing stills of it now."

Coroner Burgess followed her down the path and under the boardwalk. Getting a first look at the scene, he paused to visually inspect the dune from a distance. Then moved closer to the victim eventually using a magnifying glass to examine the exposed ankle, foot and toes. After several seconds of feeling for a pulse and without a word, he stood up and motioned for the assistants to bring the stretcher. Without acknowledging Brooke, he looked down at his phone:

"Pronounced Dead on the scene at 8:03am..."

Again, without a word to Brooke, he continued to document information via voice:

"Upon arrival, visual inspection reveals, the ankle is swollen with initial stages of ecchymosis..."

"Wait! What did you say?" Brooke interrupted the coroner. Who impatiently answered:

"The ankle has acute bruising... especially over the Anterior Talo-fibular Ligament. Musta sprained their ankle prior to the death."

Brooke looked at him in disbelief.

How does he know this after only seconds?

He finally looked up from his phone to Brooke's amazed face. She felt like a deer in headlights, unable to comprehend or respond to the information provided.

"Acute Localized Swelling doesn't happen post-mortem."

Brooke was trying to make the connection. However, must have looked perplexed because

Coroner Burgess began to speak directly to her. He spoke slowly and combined with his very clear southern drawl; he sounded more emphatic.

"Let me break it down...No heartbeat = no circulation = no swelling= no ecchymosis= no bruising." It was obvious now to both of them that she finally understood the difference between premortem verses postmortem injuries.

Can he see the lightbulb above my head?

As if to prepare for confrontation, Brooke tilted her head upward to make direct eye contact.

"This victim didn't bury herself. Someone else was here."

"No shit Sherlock," he said under this breath. She could hear the mocking sarcasm in his voice as he peered down at Brooke from his height advantage. Not to be easily intimidated, she continued,

"This is a crime scene. Before you do anything, we need to complete our on-site investigation, gather evidence..."

He cut her off immediately and unapologetically like an exotic sports car merging into perimeter I-285 Atlanta traffic.

"I'm the Elected Coroner of Charleston County, I call the shots. Gotta git dun here and git over ta Edisto for an 89 year old man, who accordin to his wife "woke up dead this morning."

Unwavering in her conviction for more time, she was not deterred by his power play followed by an attempt at humor. Instead, she pushed harder to continue to control the investigation.

"Now that Corley's finished with the stills, Detectives Howard and Daniel can collect evidence samples as they remove the sand. As soon as they have the remains fully uncovered and Corley gets a few more clicks, your team can take the lead."

"Well thank you Darlin for let'n me do my job. Tell Palmer, he's got 15 minutes."

Brooke didn't bother to explain Sergeant Palmer's medical leave. Instead, she took the 15 minutes offered, then planned to stall if she needed more time. Luckily for everyone on scene, Detectives Howard and Daniels were able to remove and bag the sand quickly. They also collected samples from the smudge and packaged the towel as evidence. Then Corley took more stills and video of the victim. It was almost an hour later before the team stepped out from under the boardwalk and motioned for Brooke to come back to the body.

"We found prints that aren't smudged. Wanted you to see them." Detective Daniels was pointing on the other post of the boardwalk.

Looks like a swirl pattern, maybe an index and thumb print.

"We collected the prints. Sending them to the Lab ASAP." It was Detective Howard. "Good job! You both are really good evidence custodians." She exited the dune and returned to the boardwalk.

Now ready to release the body to Coroner Burgess. Brooke motioned her head in acknowledgement that the deceased was ready to be removed. His team was able to relocate the victim's entire body onto the stretcher. Once on the stretcher, the body bag was zipped up, and carried up the boardwalk, and into the van. Now in privacy, the coroner unzipped the body bag to reveal the mid-thirties brown haired victim whose previously tanned skin was now pasty pale.

As Brooke and Detective Corley observed the coroner's brief examination of the body at the scene, and even though Detective Corley had good photos of the victim, Brooke wanted to commit as much of the scene to memory as possible.

Victim, laying on her left side in a fetal position with her arms and knees pulled against her body. A diagonal bruise consumed most of her upper back. A gapping wound down the middle of the bruise. Her hair was matted against the back of her mis-shapen skull. Of note are her muscular legs, with defined thigh and calf musculature visible even from this far away. Yet, her arms were slim, almost delicate looking curled up against the bony sternum. No wounds on her arms. She's only wearing a white swimsuit top as cover, leaving her arms, abdomen and back bare. Her legs were pulled up towards her chest and she wore white scalloped edge shorts. Her fingers and toes were recently manicured and painted with blue polish.

"Poor woman," Brooke whispered.

Who is this beautiful woman and how did she end up under the boardwalk?

A SC driver's license was found in the back right pocket of her shorts. Lauren Humphrey Wright from North Charleston. Born 05/23/1987. 5'-6" tall, 157 pounds. Her picture revealed an attractive woman with thick long brown curly hair and blue eyes.

Poor beautiful woman, what the heck happened to you? In the front right pocket was a single key. Brooke instructs:

"Corley, take that key as evidence and make a copy." He bagged up the key and handed it to Brooke to inspect. It was ordinary gold-tone, and worn from years of use, with no unique features.

"No cell phone?" Brooke asked.

"No phone, no car keys."

Brooke thought to herself:

Either: The victim was staying in one of the villas and came out to the beach without her phone then was murdered by a random person,

Or: The victim was murdered by someone she knew somewhere else then brought to the beach to dispose of her body.

Bottom Line: Looks like she had lots of premortem injuries.

CHAPTER 2

Ride Like the Wind Again

Three weeks earlier...
    It was like any other mondane day at the office, until Lauren Wright returned from her lunch break to find a suprise. As she entered the front door of the office, the spring bouquet of Gerbera daisies, snap dragons, and azaleas caught her attention. They were wrapped in floral paper and laying on her desk.
    Don't get excited... It's a mistake. Never gotten flowers before. It's for someone else in the office. Not for me...
    Admiring the beauty of the bright red, orange, and pink of the bouquet, she removed her jacket and placed it on the back of her chair. She could smell the fresh cut flowers as she picked them up to inspect for an intended recipient. Inside, she found an envelope.
    "Lauren Humphrey". Her heart began to palpate as she frantically sat in her swivel chair.
    I haven't been called by my maiden name in at least a decade.

Opening the envelope with excitement and reluctant curiosity, inside she found white stock paper with a handwritten note:
"Ride like the wind again!
You know where!
Sea you there!
After our Heritage.
You will regret missing this!
Your bff"

However, after reading the first line, "Ride like the wind again!" She immediately recognized the mantra from her childhood days spent riding bikes with her bff, Kathleen Rothwell. They would scream the lyrics to the Christopher Cross song incessantly every morning as they raced down the beach. She knew in her heart the flowers must be from Kathleen.

"You know where!" Must mean on the pristine beaches of Kiawah Island, SC where Kathleen's family owned a villa. The island was very exclusive due to private ownership of a majority of the land. Lauren's family was not able to afford vacations on Kiawah Island. However, She had spent every break from school with her bff, Kathleen. Surely, this "where" was the Kiawah Villa.

"Sea you there!" Obviously a play on the words See and Sea. Another hint for the beachfront Villa at Kiawah Island?

"After our Heritage." Could this Heritage be referring to the Heritage Golf Classic? If so, the Heritage is held the week after the Masters golf tournament, which Lauren realized is in three weeks! Could this clue mean to be there in three weeks? Although the note is not Kathleen's handwriting, who else could know that they had spent the week after The Heritage Golf Classic together as teens for 5 years in a row? Kathleen must have texted the message for the florist to hand write the note.

"You will regret missing this!" This sentence sounds a little strange. What could it mean? Kathleen had always been so dramatic. She must have known that Lauren was in need of a vacation, a distraction from the divorce and Donald.

Haven't seen Kathleen in how long? Must be at least 20 years. I thought that she was still holding a grudge. Gotta find a way to be there!

CHAPTER 3

Weren't Here Attol

Later the same night Donald was trying to fall asleep and could only think of how defeated he felt. While his thoughts were spinning in viscous loops, he contemplated his miserable life:

I work so hard, but never seem to get ahead. Even livin with Momma, I can't pay my bills. That court takes most of my check every damn week for child support and alimony and gives it to that Bitch. Then, the damn lawyer takes everything else. It'd be so much better if that bitch had just stayed here at my Momma's house. It would have saved me so much money. If she had just stayed here.

Almost falls asleep, but then in his slumber thinks to himself:

OR If she weren't here attol , then I wouldn't have to pay her anything! The youngins here with me and Momma. Everything, so much better...

Donald drifted off to sleep.

CHAPTER 4

Goodbye City Life

Kathleen used her manicured nails to adjust a few strands of her short, auburn hair as she pushed up from the salon chair. After re-tying the gauze belt to her flowing white maxi dress, she turned to face Margarita. Speaking in the perfect local dialect of Spanish:

"El color castano rojizo se ve maravilloso. Sin embargo, me gusta algunos flequillos mas." (The auburn color looks wonderful. However, I like some more bangs.)

Margarita was one of the friends Kathleen had made in Madrid, Spain. Within the first week of landing, she had rid herself of her signature long mane. Her short spiky hair was now easy to manage. It felt liberating after wearing long hair for so many years. Without fail, every three weeks Kathleen had maintained her auburn color and received a touch up trim. She found that during her visits to the Toni&Guy Salon over the last year had revealed wonderful insights into the culture and everyday habits of the locals. Margarita spoke English, which had been a Godsend for Kathleen when she had first arrived in Spain.

Although it's not customary to tip in Madrid, knowing that it was her last visit to the salon, Kathleen handed the stylist 100 Euros as she hugged and kissed her cheek.

"Muchas gracias, Margarita."

"Donatos señorita, Kathleen."

She could not believe that the year in Spain had come to an end. Having engrossed herself in the culture wholeheartedly, her mornings began with thoughts of pan tostada (toast) and cafe con leche (coffee with milk). The shop on the corner, Toma Cafe 1, where Kathleen had started each day was another site for excellent people-watching. It was divided into 2 areas, one with internet service which was quiet, and the other livelier side was wireless blocked. There Kathleen had befriended Marta, the barista on the non-internet side of the coffee shop and had developed many casual relationships with locals. Although she spent some time on the quiet side of the cafe, most of her mornings were spent sitting in the interactive area of the cafe that promoted conversations amongst locals and visitors to the Plaza del Dos Mayo. After enjoying her breakfast and coffee, Kathleen spent her days exploring the beautiful city, and her nights began on the rooftops of Gran Via. Where each night Kathleen took in the sunset and the culture over Madrid while sipping Tinto de Verano (red wine, soda water, lemon and ice) with Marta.

Going back to the U.S. was a little scary to

say the least. She had taken the year in Madrid after the loss of her father. Although she had been able to push the thoughts of her previous abuse to the back of her mind, now her father's cruelty began to creep in again. The mere thought of going back to the US triggered her heart to race and her palms to sweat.

Kathleen stepped out of the hair salon and onto the beautiful city sidewalk. Her driver now opened the car door and she got into the back of the sedan.

"To the airport, now Kathleen?"

"Yes, I can't put it off anymore. It is time to get back to Kiawah."

Moments later, the sedan pulled away from the curb and into traffic towards the airport.

CHAPTER 5

Jeopardy

Friday, April 14

Brooke received a response text from Joleen:
"Tags from Dawkins uploaded
No missing person report
No prior record
Husband Donald Wright.
Disorderly Conduct
Public Drunkenness
Columbia, SC. "

She notes his prior arrests for disorderly conduct and public drunkenness.

So not a saint, but not a hardened criminal either. Wonder if he had something to do with her death or even realizes that she's missing?

Brooke responded to Joleen's text with a thank you and more questions:

"TY. Going to meet the Coroner to notify the Husband.

Victim's Phone? Auto Registration?"

Next, Brooke received confirmation of the husband's address and without hesitation, began the hour and a half drive to his home. Her mind raced as she followed the Coroner along the Interstate 26 West towards Columbia. The farther from Charleston they drove, the more the area again became more rural. They exited the interstate and turned left onto a secondary road, later took a right onto the dirt road with no other cars in sight. Finally, after 2 bumpy miles down the poorly maintained dirt road, she and her dust cloud turned beside the rusted mailbox 496 into the ill-defined driveway of the small delapidated wooden home. As she made the turn, a middle aged man walked quickly out of the front door, down the concrete block steps and sprinted under the aluminum carport. He used his key fob to open the driverside door just as Brooke and the coroner pulled into the driveway blocking the man's exit. Brooke parked behind the 2023 Dodge Durango . Although not originally planning to approach Donald Wright in his front yard, Brooke now found it necessary to casually ask him to step away from the SUV for everyone's safety.

"Would you mind stepping out from under the carport? We are looking for Donald Wright." Brooke asked while standing with authority yet, remaining behind the sheild of her car door.

"Who's asking?" The figure from under the carport asked.

"Mr. Wright, Detective Brooke Mason with Charleston County PD. Are you familiar with Lauren Humphrey Wright?"

"Yes, she's my soon-to-be ex-wife. Did

she send you here? Serving me more papers?" Reluctantly, the figure moved from under the shadow of the carport and into the afternoon sun. He looked like he could use a good hair cut and was dressed in jeans and a black Def Leopard t-shirt. Brooke could see both of his hands as he walked towards her car. He looked defeated, with his rounded shoulders, however Brooke trusted no one.

"Do you mind having a seat?" Brooke motioned to the picnic table under the nearby tree.

"Just sit on top of the table, so I can see your hands. Just need to talk." Once Donald Wright was seated on the picnic table with his hands on his knees. Brooke motioned for the Richland County Coroner to get out of the car and join them near the picnic table. The coroner began.

"Mr. Wright, I'm Richland County Coroner. It is with sympathy and regret that we are here to inform you that a woman's body was found this morning… We think that it's Lauren Humphrey Wright. I'm asking you to come to the morgue to give a positive identification of her body."

Donald looked and sounded annoyed:

"Is this a joke? Can't be… Lauren is vacationing in Kiawah. I'm here takin care of the kids and Momma."

"No it's not a joke, Mr Wright. You say that Lauren was vacationing. Do you know where she was staying on Kiawah?

"No, didn't ask."

"Do you know who she was vacationing with? Or was she alone?"

"Said that it was some ole friend of hers. But I ain't buying it."

"Why not? Do you have a reason to believe that she was untruthful?" Brooke now wondered if a new flame may be involved.

"Just thinking that a good looking woman like her otta be able to catch a rich man."

"Do you have a name for this friend?"

"Kathleen's what she told me."

"Kathleen, so she was meeting a female friend? How about a last name?"

"No. Like I said, Never heard tale of this ole friend before."

"Mr. Wright, this is a serious matter. Do you mind coming down to the morgue? We do need a positive ID."

"I aint goin to no morgue. Can't do that sorta thang. Don't do…you know bodies and stuff. What happened to The B, I mean, Lauren?"

Brooke didn't want to give away any information, redirecting the conversation:

"We're not sure yet Mr. Wright. We need for you to meet us at the morgue before 8:00 pm tonight. You will be driven to the morgue by one of our officers. He will be arriving here shortly. In the mean time, we can speed up things at the morgue with a little more information. Can you tell us who her dentist was?"

"Yes, Dr. Martin Freely.. Off a Beltline Blvd.

Here in Columbia." his voice now shaking: "What happened to Lauren?"

"Mr. Wright, we will need you to come down to the morgue. An officer will be arriving at your address within the next 2 hours. We don't usually have this type of conversation here in a driveway. Just some questions to help in our investigation."

"What? Investigation? What the hell is going on?" He asked now with distress on his face and in his voice.

"Mr. Wright, please answer your front door when the officer arrives."

"What am I supposed to tell Justin and Margaret?" he trailed off.

Brooke didn't know how to answer, finally she responded.

"I'm sorry for your family's loss Mr. Wright and I really do appreciate your help. Could you tell me your wife's phone number and place of employment?"

"Yeah, sum place called Morris Tax somethin… in North Charleston, you ready for her digits?"

"Would you please text them to Officer Joleen Byrd at the number that appeared on your phone?"

"Ummm, yeah. Gonna save your contact. What's your name again?"

"Detective Brooke Mason"

"Of Kiawah Island Police Department?"

Representing only part of one barrier island had almost become a jab or a left hook to Brooke. She was part of a team of detectives much bigger than Kiawah Island. Taking the jab in stride, she answered proudly:

"No, Charleston County, Major Accident Investigation Team."

"Got it. Fixin to send the digits now...803 555-1212 done."

Wanting more information on the victim's relationship with her soon to be ex-husband, Brooke tried to gently pry more.

"So, your wife was working in North Charleston and living in Columbia? That's a two hour commute."

"No, she up and moved out, took our youngins with her... Divorce supposed to happen in 3 weeks."

"Was she living with anyone in North Charleston?"

"Naw, Don't think so, Rivers Avenue's all I know. Mandatory meetup's in Orangeburg. Never been to the place in North Charleston."

"In the morning, I'll need you to meet me at the Charleston County Police Station on Lockwood at 9 am to help in our investigation. By the way, Mr. Wright, when was the last time that you spoke to Lauren Wright?"

"Two days ago, when I picked up Justin and Maggie in Orangeburg, you know off of I-26 at the Hardee's Restaurant."

"Thank you for your help, Mr. Wright. I will see you in the morning at 9am. An officer will escort you to the morgue tonight. Goodbye."

Brooke got into her car, and backed out of the driveway and began the 2 mile long journey down the front alignment destroying dirt road.

You can see that dust cloud for miles. She thought as she parallel parked across the street from the intersection of the dirt road and the paved secondary road. Prepared for a short stake out, she took out the yeti and sipped cold water.

From here, I can see him leave from a mile away. That dusty road.

Next, she sends a text to Detective Howard with her coordinates:

Meet me here.

Near the husband's home.

Prepared for stakeout then

escort to Morgue before 8pm.

Now lets see how Mr. Wright reacts to his new information...Detective Howard will know how to read this guy.

Brooke waited until Howard's arrival before making the trip back to the Kiawah crime scene. She had given him vague instructions:

"Once you get there...Dont be in a hurry, check out the place, get a feel for him...Do your thing, make that connection. Wait for Donald Wright to slip up...Catch him in a lie..."

Donald watched as the coroner and the

officer backed out of the driveway. Thinking back to the meet up with Lauren, Donald suddenly felt overwhelming worry. He remembered driving away from the Hardee's in Orangeburg with Justin and Margaret in the back seat of his new SUV. He had given Lauren one of his best looks: "the eat shit and die" in the rear view mirror. His thoughts had been racing with rage:

Can't believe she thinks that she has the money to spend time on an island like Kiawah for an entire week. Been draining me dry with alimony and child support for the last year going through the divorce. Then 3 weeks before our court date she goes on vacation? And who is this childhood friend that I've never met? Where is she getting all this money? Me?! Or maybe she has a new rich man in her life.

The thought of Lauren moving on with her life didn't bother Donald as much as her taking and spending <u>his</u> money. The more that Donald thought about it, the angrier he became.

She has no right to take money from me and spend it on stupid Kiawah Beach vacations. And she's gonna be getting it til Justin turns 18… ten more years.

Still lost in a circling thought of frustration, Donald stopped in front of the unkept home which could use a good cleaning and an update. He opened the rusted mailbox door, gathered all of the letters, and began to flip through. He noticed a letter addressed to Lauren Wright among the stack and it infuriated him further:

Why didn't she change her address with her boss? In 3 weeks, I'm gonna be FORCED into paying alimony and child support for the next... however long that damn judge says. How's she able to afford Kiawah Island, the "rich people island" in the lowcountry?

Still holding the envelope in his hand:

Well, Momma can deal with gittin it to her.

Donald continued to flip through and retrieved all of his mail: three past due notices and a car magazine. Placing the past due notices into the center console, he turned to his phone enthralled children, Justin and Margaret.

"We're home. Put away your damn phones and go hug your Gramma, Marilyn."

Donald walked into the kitchen door and placed the rest of the mail on the kitchen countertop for his mother to find. Then he went to the refrigerator and opened the door and grabbed a Natural Light, pulled the aluminum tab and took a long drink of the ice-cold beer.

Just what I need..

Feeling glad to have a cold beer, until he remembered his actions from the night before.

"Oh shit!".

Flashback
Thursday, April 13

Donald stood up from the table stretching, began to clear the plates and turned to his mother:

"Momma, your chicken fried steak's blue

ribbon, the best in state. And love your Mac and cheese too! Thank you for supper. You're a good Momma." he said, kissing her on the cheek.

"and the best Gramma. Justin and Maggie never eat like this when Lauren cooks. You go on and rest now. I'll take care of the dishes."

Donald turned toward Justin and Margaret

"Thank your Gramma for supper. Time for a bath, go upstairs. See you when you're clean."

He gathered dishes and walked into the kitchen, noticed today's mail, still sitting on the countertop untouched. He grabbed a large mug, filled it with water, and placed it in the microwave. Then, he returned to the sink of dishes. As Donald was waiting for the water to boil, he rinsed dishes and loaded the dishwasher. When the microwave rang, he pulled on gloves, and picked up the envelope addressed to Lauren H Wright. He reached for the utensil drawer and pulled out a butter knife. Then held the butter knife and the flap over the steam and gently tried to open the envelope from one side.

Damn, this always works the first time in the movies...

Not enough steam.

He started a pot of water on the stove. Went back to the sink and began to wash the silverware, as loudly as possible, ensuring that no one would enter the kitchen to disturb his secret mission.

No one will want to help with doing dishes.

Returning to the stove, the water now

began to evaporate into steam. Again, he warmed the butter knife and the envelope seal over the steam. This time it was working better and it looked like one more time would do the trick. He slid the warm butter knife between the envelope and the flap, guiding it along the glued edge.

Not perfect, but it worked.

He looked at the small tears on the envelope flap:

Things get damaged in shipping all the time. No one will notice once it's glued back.

Finally, with the flap open, he gently pulled the folded papers out expecting information about her pay or taxes. However, it was neither, instead there was a letter and a form. The title at the top of the form said: "Change of Beneficiary" and had all of Lauren's life insurance information. However, it had not been signed or the new designee completed. Not only had she not changed her address, Lauren had not changed her beneficiary on her life insurance policy.

So stupid. Forgot to do the paperwork?

Wearing gloves, Donald folded the papers, returned them to the envelope, pressed the seal closed with some Elmer's glue and returned it to the middle of today's mail stack on the kitchen countertop for his mother to find.

Donald finished loading the dishwasher, cleaned the counters and then joined his Momma in the living room.

"Donnie, See if you can answer the final

Jeopardy question."

"What's the category?"

"Exploration"

"Alright, I can try this one. Do you bet everything, half or nothing based on the category." This evens the odds for Donald. They have pretended for years that going into final Jeopardy. They are tied at $10,000. In Donald's mind there are only 3 options, all based on him missing the answer.

"I think that we both have a chance on this one. I'm betting it all."

"You have more confidence in me than I do. I'm betting half."

The familiar music of Jeopardy final question begins as the "answer" is displayed on Marilyns old "non-smart" television:

"James Cook's account of a 1774 visit here records an object "near 27 feet long and upwards of 8 foot over the breast or shoulders."

Donald thinks: *What!? Really!? What kind of clue is that? I have no idea. Ok fast, say something."*

The Jeopardy theme song ends. And Donald makes his guess:

"The sphinx? That's my answer. Ok Momma, what's your answer?"

"Easter island." Marilyn answers confidently.

Jeopardy answer: What is Easter Island?

"$20,000 for you, Momma! $5,000 for me. You win!"

As the Jeopardy music played in the background, they both smiled glad that she had won. They sat in silence for the rest of the evening as she read a book and he looked for old girlfriends on social media.

Donald's thoughts drift away from the day of Lauren's death and now return to his present dilemma of needing an alibi.

Good thing my Momma can vouch for me.

CHAPTER 6

Pink Whales and Safety Pins

Friday, April 14

Brooke answered her phone to hear Joleen whispering in her twangy southern drawl:

"Hey, I'm not supposed to say anything yet but..." long dramatic pause in Joleen's voice. "You didn't hear this from me Brooke. But, her shorts had that pink whale logo, you know, Vineyard Vines." Joleen almost whispers.

"And inside the waist was one of those little tiny safety pins. You know the kind... with the string for the price tag. Musta been brand new. Gotta go!" The call ends.

Brooke sends an unofficial text back
"TY!".

Then more questions:

"Did you get the victim's phone number? Ping?"

At least now, I have a lead to start tracing her last steps. Freshfields Village has a place that sells the pink whale stuff. But gonna need a favor from Corley.

Brooke runs to catch up to Detective Micheal Corley, now packing his car with photography equipment.

"Hey Corley, Autopsy's tonight at 8. I'm gonna need you there for the external exam."

"I thought that it would be quick. Yeah, I'll be there." Corley responds, still packing his equipment into the trunk of his car.

"Good! Now a favor…" Brooke begins. He looks up curiously.

"Head to the coroner's office now. See if you can get some stills of her clothing and any tags or name brands… and then send images to me? Got a lead on a known location and don't want to wait 'til after the autopsy to get started."

"Sure thing. I'm all in on this one, Brooke." Now able to smile for the first time today, they make eye contact. Friends for the last 8 years since graduating from the academy, they both remove the professional persona.

"Working with you and Joleen, my two favorite officers, on my very first Lead Investigation. I can't believe that it's happening. And I'm scared of screwing this up bigtime!"

"You got this Brooke. If you don't believe in yourself, then trust in me. You are the best qualified officer to fill in for Palmer during his medical leave."

"Thank you! I owe you! Oh! Yeah! Get pictures of toenail polish too if you can!"

"You're welcome. Lead Investigator, Detective Brooke Mason," Corley said with a grin. Brooke smiled back thankful for Corley's encouragement. She knew that his words were genuine. As she hastily walked to her SUV, she thought:

Corley, I do trust your judgment.

CHAPTER 7

EXES, MILS & CPAS - Oh My!
Wednesday, April 12

Lauren started the one hour trip to Orangeburg to meet with her soon to be ex-husband, Donald, to drop off their 2 children, Justin and Margaret. Now driving, she began to think about her life and court date for her divorce to be finalized was three weeks away.

Boy, I need a vacation. How long has it been since I've been alone for more than a couple of nights? At least a decade? Over a decade.

Can't believe that we were married for 12 years. Knew when I married Donald... that he withheld information (lied) and liked to drink a few beers. But I really believed him, when he told me that it would get better once we were married. Instead, the drinking and lying got much worse and created financial problems. Lost in thought, she remembered the beginning of the end:

Two years ago, they lost their home when Donald lost his job. It had started when he became angry after having too much to drink. Something about a parking spot in the downtown

Columbia, SC five points area and an asshole who stole it. The foot patrol police were on the scene quickly when they heard Donald's profanity from down the street. As he was being arrested, things spiraled out of control when he resisted the officers. He was held for and plead guilty to disorderly conduct. Unable to raise bail, he lost his job forcing the family of four to move in with Donald's momma, Marilyn. The tiny dilapidated home felt unwelcome to Lauren. She had tried to make the new living arrangement work. Not caving to Marilyn's unhealthy cooking style, Lauren made healthy lunches for children to balance the southern fried dinners that Marilyn prepared. However, She felt that her parenting style was continuously scrutinized by Marilyn. Donald always found a way to turn things around and make it sound like it was Lauren's fault. Within three months, she could no longer take it and secretly made a plan to take the children and move out. She brushed up on her bookkeeping skills and got a job and began to stash money away from Donald. After a year of saving and continuing to endure her unfulfilled marriage, Lauren informed Donald that she had leased an apartment in North Charleston, on Rivers Avenue and would be moving on January 3.

    Lauren smiled as she remembered the first night in her own place, no furniture, no Donald, just the Margaret, Justin and me. Not located in a touristy side of Charleston like rainbow row or the Market: Rivers Avenue in North Charleston had once been an industrial area supplying the nearby Naval Shipyard. After the shipyard closed in 1996, much of the area was abandoned. However, in recent years it had undergone revitalization, with the addition of middle income homes, apartments and retail stores moving back into the area. Lauren had been excited and proud to "have her own place near the beach".

Ok, it's really kinda near the beach, about 45 minutes on a great traffic day. The last mile along the coast may take another 45 minutes. Then another 15 to find parking. But it's my place, near-ish the beach! She smiled, so very proud of herself. For the first time, at the age of 36, Lauren Humphrey Wright had a place of her own.

Her thoughts now returned back to her current meet up with Donald, she took exit 145 off of Interstate 26 and turned left into the Hardee's Restaurant parking lot. Before she parked, she said out loud to Justin and Margaret who were engrossed in their phones.

"I'm going to miss both of you! I love you!"

"Love you too, Momma." said Justin as he looked up from his phone realizing the car had stopped. Margaret soon followed with

"Love you, keep your phone close in case I need you."

"I will." Lauren answered. Thinking

When you are a teenager, it will be <u>me</u> asking <u>you</u> to keep your phone close in case I need you.

She hugged and kissed both children while Donald took their duffel bags and belongings out of the trunk of Lauren's car and placed them in his new Dodge Durango. He closed the trunk and proclaimed:

"Time to go kids, we have over an hour drive home."

"Have fun at your Grandma's house." Justin and Margaret climbed into the back seat of the new Dodge Durango amazed at the contrast from the decade old Honda Accord. Donald answered in a sarcastic judgemental tone:

"Yeah! Party it up on yer expensive vacation with yer 'old friend'".

Without another word, Donald got into the Durango and drove away looking at Lauren in the rear view mirror.

Donald is such an ass! This is exactly why I need this vacation.

She wanted to feel free of everything in her life, to liberate herself from the constant judgment of her ex-husband, the recent confrontation with her employer's 24 year old granddaughter, and the pure exhaustion of raising children.

On the drive back to her apartment Lauren began to think back to her discoveries at the tax and accounting firm. Lost in thought, Lauren develops a pit in the bottom of her stomach as she begins to remember…three weeks earlier.

Tuesday, March 21

While completing the February ledger audit for her employer, Morris Tax and Accounting, Lauren had noticed discrepancies. Although she was not an accountant, she did have bookkeeping experience.

This is driving me crazy! I must have missed something.

She had accepted the position of administrative assistant in January of this year. Her duties include posting receipts and deposits into the ledger. While doing so, Lauren noticed discrepancies between the ledger and the February statement. She refreshed the spreadsheet and recalculated the data.

Nope, still doesn't add up, she looked at the $53,324.86 difference on the February spreadsheet.

I know that I entered everything correctly.

Then Lauren has another thought:

Maybe, I'm not the problem.

She opened the January spreadsheet and scrolled down to the month end information.

Oh. Here it is.

Noting the obvious discrepancy between the bank statement and the ledger data for January.

A difference of $33,000. Crazy. No way, exact numbers like that don't happen.

She opened the spreadsheet for last year, and scrolled to the year end financials.

Maybe, the firm carried over the discrepancy

from Q4 last year.

Upon reviewing the numbers, she discovered $118,324.87 missing from last year. Each time Lauren compared the spreadsheet to the ledger for last year, she came up short $118,324.87.

She returned to the January and February spreadsheets and summed the two months.

$86,593.68 missing for Quarter one so far this year.

Lauren, now with a completion complex, followed the money trail backwards, enjoying the feeling an engineer gets when reverse engineering a product, or a detective putting together clues to solve a mystery. She continued her investigative research, opening financials for previous years. However, she did not find any discrepancies. Continuing to snoop over the rest of the week, she found her answer and did not like the result. All roads lead back to Jennifer Morris, the frail looking 24 year old third generation tax accountant granddaughter of the firm's founder.

Based on the financial data, I bet that Jennifer started working at her family firm in June of last year. That's when the discrepancies began.

Once Lauren was absolutely sure, she copied the financial evidence onto a USB drive and sent a text to Jennifer.

"How about a quick lunch today at noon? 6907 Rivers Ave. N. Char."

Lauren chose a public location that would still allow a private conversation; Sitting in her parked car outside of a taco truck was the perfect solution. Still remembering that day three weeks ago, she had been happy that Jennifer agreed immediately to the lunch meet-up. They did meet outside of the taco truck. However, things didn't go as Lauren had planned. She chose to push the memory out of her mind, now pulling into her parking space at the apartment.

CHAPTER 8

Roundabout 12 Minutes

My very own parking space, she proudly thought, then reminded herself to focus on vacation. Lauren began to get ready for her trip to Kiawah. She could not pass up the opportunity for a break from her stressful life. Suddenly, the perfect opportunity for a pleasant diversion had presented itself to her in the most dramatic way, flowers and a note. The opportunity to use Kathleen's family's Kiawah Island golf villa for the week sounded wonderful. She began to daydream about her upcoming trip. Lauren packed two swimsuits with cover ups and dreamed about the evening swim that she would take tonight.

Can't believe that it's finally here. Tonight, I'm definitely gonna swim... in the pool at the resort or the ocean. How long has it been? How many years since she had been to a pool? Any pool? Maybe 3? Definitely gonna be nice to swim in an adult pool...while being served a cold adult beverage...I wonder if Kathleen will be there for the week, or if I have the entire place to myself.

She continued to pack while recalling all of

the wonderful places to ride her bike. She knew that it was easy to rent a bike, or have tennis or golf lessons while on Kiawah. She was excited to take her own bike for the first time. Now to pack for the beach bike ride, she packed white tennis shoes, denim shorts, and midriff tank top. Of course, beaches are so casual that Lauren could wear anything. She paused for a moment remembering the beach.

Kiawah Island is the most beautiful beach that I've ever seen. Perfect for riding bikes, compact soil, wide open spaces and very few obstacles to interrupt your path. Riding on Kiawah Island beach is like having your very own paradise.

Lauren took a moment to picture herself on the beach riding her bike. She closed her eyes, took a deep slow breath, held it then slowly blew it out, while visualizing inhaling the beach and exhaling all her stress.

For her visit to the Sanctuary, Kiawah Island's most exclusive resort, she packed a collared shirt and khaki shorts, for the more upscale dress code. Located at the far end of the island, the resort is surrounded by one of the most beautiful golf courses in the country, the Ocean Course. The bike ride to the Sanctuary was her favorite ride on the beach. Every part of the golf course is so immaculately pristine. Many avid golfers said it compares to the Augusta National Golf course where the Masters is played or to the Pebble Beach course on the west coast. Again, she closed her eyes, took a slow deep breath, imagined the Ocean Course and slowly exhaled.

For her John's Island ride, she packed bike shorts and a sports tank. John's Island is extremely casual; it's more like the everyday middle class person's island experience. Then for comfort, Lauren packed some mom jeans, a pair of Capri pants, a couple of t-shirts, and threw in some lounge pants and PJ's. Lastly, she decided on a hanging bag to pack a spring floral maxi dress and short blazer for the upscale dining available on Kiawah Island.

You never know what Kathleen will want to do. Just in case...

Later that morning, Lauren loaded her car with her suitcase and garment bag, attached her bike to the rack, then began her vacation. The drive from her apartment in North Charleston to Kiawah Island was an easy 45 minutes, not requiring her to use any navigation. She knew the way: take I-26 East, Exit onto Hwy 17 Savannah Hwy, Left onto Main Road to the turnabout, then exit towards Kiawah Island. It was a busy traffic day. As she approached the left on Main Rd. Listening to the song with the intent to relax and be in the moment, she opened the sunroof and turned up the volume on the car stereo. She began to sing:

"It's a bright, bright, sunny day…" By the end of the song, Lauren was beginning to melt into vacation mode. Next on the radio is Bob Marley's song Three Little Birds, Lauren continued to sing:

"Don't worry 'bout a thing. 'Cause every little thing is gonna be alright".

She let out a slow sigh of relief as she drove through the intersection.

Not long now!

The two-lane road was riddled with potholes and repaired areas on the blacktop. The obstacles of holes were spaced perfectly apart to make hitting each and every one unavoidable. The bumpy road intensified every squeaky piece of plastic on the dash of her decade old car. Lauren increased the volume and sang the song louder.

"Woke up this morning, smiled with the rising sun!"

In the morning, I will be smiling at the rising sun on Kiawah as I "Ride like the wind again," but first I need a pedicure.

As Lauren approached the Roundabout she decreased the volume on the stereo. Then, exited the roundabout towards Seabrook Island.

Off to The Kiawah Nail Salon for a long overdue pedicure and some relaxing "me" time.

CHAPTER 9

Liquid Courage and Crawdads

Thursday, April 13

Kathleen took the last sip of her drink, and wished she had something stronger.

I've been dreading going back to Kiawah for the last year! Can't believe I'm doing it now.

She made eye contact with the flight attendant and held up her empty glass.

Father is gone, dead, buried. It's over...Then why am I so anxious?

Thank goodness that there is still time for another drink before the jet taxis down the runway for takeoff. Two drinks before lunch. She thought, then justified it to herself.

Mimosas shouldn't count for anything. Champagne and orange juice offer little in the form of liquid courage.

Kathleen always traveled first class, and expected great service. For today's trans-atlantic flight, she had purchased an extra seat for her two dog carriers. Thank goodness that there was no one sitting beside her. She didn't like to chit chat on the plane, instead she distracted herself with the movie: Where the Crawdads Sing. She remembered and looked forward to seeing the beautiful marsh along the South Carolina Coast.

She embraced the theme of the movie:

"Creatures do what they must to survive."

The images and language began to ease her into her more traditional low country mindset. As she made her way back to the US, she began to think in American English with a Charleston based Southern Draw again (pronounced agin).

CHAPTER 10

Snorts and Sprouts

Thursday, April 13

Feeling much more relaxed after her mani/pedi, Lauren smiled as she spotted the Co-op Cafe across the street from the nail salon. Reading the advertisement in the window:

> *" A Peach Froze'*
> *made from wine*
> *served frozen and*
> *"Available to go."*
> *The perfect beach drink."*

Just what I need to get into vacation mode.

She crossed the beautifully landscaped street of the perfect "pre-planned village" and headed to the cafe. Once inside the sandwich shop, with the wonderful smells of food surrounding her, Lauren realized she had not eaten all day and it was approaching 2 pm.

I'll order lunch to eat on the sidewalk table and two peach froze' to go. Kathleen and I will enjoy those later today on the beach.

She placed her order and walked out to the sidewalk. There she found a cute wrought iron cafe table topped with a black and white striped umbrella. It was a great place to continue to absorb the landscape of the perfect little vacation town, Freshfields Village. Thinking of the wonderful fresh ingredients, she waited for the turkey sandwich on toasted whole grain bread served with avocado, lettuce, tomato, and alfalfa sprouts. While daydreaming about her sandwich and absorbing the perfectly manicured flowers along the sidewalk, someone caught her eye. Down the side street, she saw a fair skinned man with long dark brown hair walking towards her table. He continued staring at her until Lauren began to feel uncomfortable.

Could you stare any harder?

The man stared straight back at her then broke into a huge grin and called her name

"Lauren! Hey! Lauren Humphrey."

He waved his hand from a few yards away as he continued toward her. Suddenly, she registered who this was.

"Kathleen told me that you may come for a getaway this week but I never believed that you would actually show up!"

It was Kathleen's younger brother, JJ. Formerly the pain in the butt and tag along, who begged to be included during each visit to Kiawah.

"JJ! My goodness! I didn't expect to see you!"

"I can't believe that I'm here either! Is

Kathleen back at the Villa?" Lauren asked.

"I'm not sure. Haven't been to the Villa yet myself. I'm heading there now. Do you want to bypass the registration desk? I can let you inside."

JJ gave a reassuring smile as he pulled the keys out of his pocket and jingled them. Then he continued to speak without pause:

"I have a spare key to the villa that I can give you to use this week."

Starting her vacation sooner sounded wonderful. She nodded her head, flashed a smile.

"That would be wonderful! Thanks JJ."

Turning his gaze away from her shyly, He gestured for her to start eating.

"I just ate an hour ago. I'm good. Call me Jay now."

She took a bite of her sandwich, then whispered,

"OMG, this is so good! I miss the delicious fresh food that rich people eat. So much better than fast food and food trucks." She began to eat her wonderfully prepared sandwich. Still looking away, Jay quickly turned to face Lauren with a more serious look and began again.

"In a few days, the villa will require bluetooth activation from my device to lock and unlock the doors. The key will be obsolete." He continued "The Villa is being remodeled and updated with a new security system. I came into town this morning to check out the contractor's work. I can't wait to see it. You know my sister,

Kathleen is updating the villa while vacationing in Spain. She expects me to see that everything is to her standards. The contractor claims that it's basically ready."

"Basically?" Lauren interjected between bites of her sandwich.

"As of this morning, everything is ready for a walk through. Except for the installation of the security system. It's going to take a few days longer. Waiting on a shipment of a motherboard or something."

"Wow, And yes! Your sister has always had expectations of perfection. I can't wait to see the villa again. Are you sure that the villa is ready to use?"

"We are gonna find out now. But I've been promised that it's ready to occupy."

JJ shrugged his shoulders then awkwardly reached up to run his hand through his shiny long dark brown hair. To Lauren, JJ had always appeared frail as a child. His fair complexion in contrast to his dark hair looked unusual to her. Plus little JJ had a slim, some would call lanky, body. He had always been a background feature in Lauren's memories. Yet here he was sitting in front of her. She could hardly believe that "Little JJ" had grown up to be Jay, such a handsome man. She gave a 100 megawatt smile, showing her two dimples and restrained her laugh:

"See you there in a dozen minutes!" They both giggled out loud. Jay responded

"Yes, we will be on the beach until the Green Sunset Song...." he trailed off. At which point, they both snickered out loud. Lauren, still laughing, "snorted" just as her plate was removed from the table and replaced with a bag containing her two peach froze'. Both hearing the snort at such an inopportune time, laughed harder as they walked away from each other towards their cars.

CHAPTER 11

So Far Away

What were you thinking? Why would you bring three children to the airport?!

The thirty something year-old woman with three children was walking down the center of the terminal making it difficult for Kathleen get around the lively family. She attempted to cut between the woman and the child to her right. At the exact same moment, the mother threw her personal bag over her shoulder, smacking Kathleen in head, and knocking her off balance. Unable to correct for the push, Kathleen fell into the oldest child of about 6. The child immediately lost grip of the cholate milkshake, splattering the contents of the cup onto the front of Kathleen's shirt. As Kathleen shrieked from the cold milkshake, The woman stumbled as she brushed past her attempting to retrieve the toddler. Numerous large carry-ons were left piled on the switchback of the serpentine belt. Kathleen was unable to move forward and was forced to wait for the mother to return with her screaming child.

Now steadily making her way through the

airport, her mind began to whirl with happy thoughts of Kiawah Island. As she neared her destination, she thought of the peaceful bike trails thought the community. There are over 30 miles of paved paths connecting every part of the island. Kathleen looked forward to the quiet beauty of the bike trails. She had rented a bike in advance for the week and now her thoughts turned to riding:

Can't wait to have the feeling of being completely alone. Wind in my face, focused on nature. Uninterrupted thoughts. Can't wait to ride along Kiawah Island Parkway. People there have manners. People in airports have no manners! Simple bike etiquette would be great in an airport! Everybody keeps to the right. Announce yourself when approaching from behind. Pass on the left. If so inclined, greet the passerby: "Good morning or How ya doin?" AND keep moving. Can't imagine how much smother life would be...if everyone followed bike etiquette.

After waiting in the serpentine line for US customs, finally, it was her turn, Kathleen handed over the passport to the TSA agent. He studied it, looked her in the eyes, then handed it back. Kathleen continued through customs with very little hold up, reaping the benefits of traveling on the redeye.

Oh! Cant wait to ride on the beach too! When is low tide? I'll search it before take off. I'd be wonderful to get a ride in today. So nice to ride on the firm sand of the lowering tide.

Deep in thought about her bike ride, she walked down the terminal and stopped to look at the updated monitor.

ATL to CHS DELAYED.

"You have got to be f-ing kidding me!" Kathleen could not believe her luck. She was caught off guard by a child's voice:

"Mom, here's that... what did you call her... id-e-ot?" It was the 6 year-old from earlier, curiously looking up to make eye contact with Kathleen. At which hearing the word "idiot" the two younger children and the mother stopped in thier tracks. Quickly the younger turned their heads to see the "idiot". While the mother attempted to gather her children without making eye contact. The family had almost cleared themselves when the child spoke again...

"I just want to see what one looks like..."

"Mathew, Stop talking and come here."

"Next time, I see one..."

Mathew, over here, Now!

Too tired to care...I flew from Spain, halfway around the world without any problems, arrived in Atlanta and can't get to Charleston. So close, yet so far away.

Kathleen turned to her entourage of baggage managers and demanded:

"Take me to the SkyMiles Club."

CHAPTER 12

Watchin Me

Jay drove away in his Tesla ecstatic with the encounter with Lauren.

She hasn't changed a bit. Her smile, her laugh, even the little snort. All just as I can still very distinctly remember... what a natural beauty. It's etched into my brain.

Jay had secretly recorded Lauren on the beach in a video on his Nokia 6600, 20 years ago when she was 17 years old. He had watched the video and listened to her laugh hundreds of times over the last 20 years. He could not believe that within minutes, he would be with her again.

Caught off guard and devastated when Lauren didn't show up for their Heritage week 19 years ago, he had asked about her over dinner with his family, however he had been met with silence. Some sort of spat between she and Kathleen. Later, Jay was devastated again when she married someone as ordinary as Donald Wright 12 years ago. Kathleen had received the wedding invitation and announced that she would be unable to attend. Jay had taken a picture of the invitation and secretly crashed the reception. He couldn't resist the opportunity to see Lauren again. Jay told himself that he was going to the reception to give himself closure to the crush. However, once there, he was unable to approach her. He watched her from afar and remained out of sight for about 30 minutes, then quietly exited the reception without speaking to anyone. Afterwards, he had lost touch with Lauren. Then eight years ago, he saw her announcement on social media after the birth of her second child, Margaret. For the last 8 years, Jay has quietly observed Lauren through social media. Every year, Jay had seen pictures of Justin's and Margaret's birthday parties. Occasionally, Jay saw family cookouts, trips to the park, and children's achievements. However, for the last year, Jay saw nothing. Then on February 14 of this year, she posted on social media that she didn't receive flowers or candy for Valentine's Day. She had pinned a location in North Charleston, Morris Tax and Accounting, 2121 Rivers Avenue. Jay looked at the location on Google Earth. Obviously, the address was an office building. Next, an internet search easily found a contact number. On February 15, Jay called the office with the intention of pretending to verify employment. However, Jay immediately recognized Lauren's voice when she answered the phone. Jay, unable to speak, immediately ended the call. Today, he was delighted that he had found the courage to have a conversation with Lauren and that he would be spending more time with her over the next week.

CHAPTER 13

She's a Keeper

Lauren drew in a deep breath and slowly exhaled as she thought of the beautiful drive that lay ahead. The drive from the roundabout to the Villa was 12 minutes. It was an old inside joke between Lauren and Kathleen as teenagers. Kathleen's mother would call to say: "See you there in a dozen minutes." It was just enough time to "Ride like the wind" back to the beach access #16 just outside of the villa. Then Kathleen, JJ and Lauren would sit on the blue beach chairs and act as if they had been there all along.

The weather was perfect, she opened the sunroof and windows of her car and began to drive towards the resort. Once again, she entered the roundabout between the three islands. This time, she exited towards Kiawah Island. Again, she took in a deep breath through her nose and out of her mouth. The wonderful smell of the marsh and the ocean air were like a drug for Lauren. More relaxation poured through her body. The winding road from the perfectly organized and maintained Freshfields Village on Seabrook Island to the Villa on Kiawah Island followed along the marsh with sea grass on the left and a forest of pine trees on the right. She pulled up to the guard, a large round man with short arms, at the gate just as Jay's Tesla pulled away.

"Guest Pass for Lauren H Wright please."

"Got it here. The Owner requested it less than a minute ago. Usually when that happens, the guest parking pass is for overnight. This Owner requested your pass for a week. I guess that means that you are a "keeper".

The guard smiled at Lauren as he compared her SC driver's license photo to the name on the guest list. Then handed her back the ID and her bright yellow parking pass.

"Welcome to Kiawah! Have a wonderful visit."

The speed limit dramatically changed after the guarded entrance. The 20 mph speed limit allowed the small paved pristinely maintained trail to wind through the inlet creeks and tall pine trees, revealing small glimpses of immaculate golf courses and bike trails.

It's like nowhere else on earth. So Peaceful!

Lauren looked down the drive along the forest lined with live oaks reaching across the top of the road. In some stretches, the live oak branches touched each other to create a natural tunnel. As she entered the Live Oak tunnel, she felt zen for the first time in almost two decades.

CHAPTER 14

Zen Retriever

Wayne Shealy
Flashback
Thursday, April 13

I can't believe that I'm going to Kiawah Island for a 3-day work conference. Aah! What a wonderful place to get away from meetings with anxiety filled clients, away from my very overly involved wife, my hormonal teenage daughter, and the expectations of life! Not only can I take my dog, Tyler: Step #1 of The Wayne and Tyler 10 Step Plan, I get to do it on a secluded beach!

As Wayne drove his 2023 black on black Toyota Highlander with all the bells and whistles, he glanced to the passenger seat and smiled at the sight of Tyler beside him. Wayne reflected on Tyler, his six year old golden retriever and recalled adopting him when his daughter, Ginger was nine years old. She begged for a pet dog for months, using every opportunity to talk about how she would feed, walk, train, brush, wash and clean up after a pet. Unfortunately, motivation is fleeting, and Wayne soon had to care for the puppy.

"Dad, would you please feed Tyler? I'm doing my math homework." Ginger would ask.

Within weeks, Tyler looked to me for breakfast each morning, ecstatic to hear me enter the kitchen to make coffee. Those puppy dog eyes looking at me, looking through me and into my soul. Tyler accepts me with all of my flaws, he respects me. By the time he was six months old, Tyler became my dog and I was Tyler's person. When Tyler turned two years old, although still a puppy, he could follow basic commands: sit, stay, lay down. Now after over five years of our trusting relationship, Tyler and I have a deep mutual connection and the same love of beautiful women. Wayne smiled as he scratched Tyler's ears.

"Right Tyler, we both love beautiful women!" Wayne reached to the dash and changed the input to FM, increased the volume, and stopped on a local radio station. He began to sing

"Woke up this morning, smiled with the rising sun!" Wayne exited the interstate and turned onto Savannah highway. He continued left at Main Road and drove for about 17 miles through the low country to the turnabout and exited toward Kiawah Island parkway. They parked at the villa and immediately stepped onto the boardwalk.

"Wow!" The beach was even more beautiful than Wayne had expected. Light gray sand, with at least 50 yards of flat beach from the dunes to the water. At low tide, the beach stretched to at least

100 yards, with miles of beach to the left and to the right. The occasional vacationer had lots of space this time of year, in order to feel secluded on the beach. He walked a little ways past the dunes, set up his beach chair, placed his wedding band in his swimsuit pocket, sat down, and peered out at the ocean, eyes squinting. Tyler sat in front of Wayne and faced straight ahead at the ocean, nose and ears sticking up, as if he was mesmerized by the vastness of it all. It was a great place to be alone, a refuge from everything and everyone who was a stressor. Here with Tyler, Wayne felt zen.

Tyler gets it. He understands me and respects me.

CHAPTER 15

Bruce Banner Margaritas

As Kathleen sat in the Atlanta Skymile Club Member Lounge, she became more self absorbed as time passed. The two Yorkshire Terrier emotional pet support animals were not providing enough support to calm her nerves. Her anxiety becoming more debilitating as the time slowly passed, and unable to relax, she ordered a second Margarita and texted her brother, Jay.

"ATL/CHS delayed! Can you believe that this is happening to me?!!"

He answered immediately.

"Oh no! Sorry Sis! Will you make it for sunset at The Salty Dog?"

"Hopefully! You know they never tell you anything except that it's delayed. Are you at the villa? How does it look?"

"Yes! Looks good. Everything as expected. Let me know when you board the plane. I'll have the driver ready at baggage claim in CHS to retrieve your luggage and bring you straight to Bohicket Marina for sunset."

"TY Jay! You know me. I am a nervous

wreck. I hate flying! Not being in control and not being a part of the plan… triggers all of my adrenaline to kick in…" She sent a gif of the mild mannered Bruce Banner turning into the Hulk; Not the recent movie superhero Hulk… the 70s TV series Hulk followed by:

"Don't make me angry!" Immediately she texted again: "Kathleen transforms into that angry redhead in first class".

"You're so good at it, why stop now?! Are you drinking?"

"How did you know? Just a margarita to celebrate being back in the US."

"I know you… please don't show up shit-faced. I have a surprise. You don't want to miss this!"

"Trying! I will text you at take- off."

Sitting on the barstool, now dressed in a short skirt and a long jacket, alone in the beautiful private lounge, Kathleen, turned toward the expectant bartender and pushed the empty glass away.

"Another margarita please."

She began her indeterminate wait time in the airport.

CHAPTER 16

Disc-us-ions

Thursday, April 13

Later that afternoon, Lauren rode her bike along the shore line in awe of the beauty of the beach. Noticing a starfish in her path, she stopped to gently help it back to its ocean home. As she returned to her bike, she could hear a dog barking and running along the beach. She glanced down the beach to see a golden retriever playing frisbee with his owner. The dog was enjoying his day as much as she was enjoying hers. As the retriever ran down the wide open beach towards the neon orange disc, he appeared to glide through the air. With apparent ease he caught the frisbee. But instead of returning to his owner, the handsome dog chose to befriend Lauren and ran up to her wagging his tail. Immediately, she dropped to one knee and started to pet the golden dog and scratch his floppy ears.

"What's your name?" Lauren asked. From behind her, she heard an answer.

"Tyler. He's Tyler. I'm Wayne." He was slightly out of breath.

"Hi Tyler!" Lauren said, then stood up and to faceTyler's person:

"And, Hi Wayne. I'm Lauren." She made contact with Wayne's very light hazel eyes and their eye contact lingered.

Wow ! He's a looker: curly dark blonde hair, tan skin and an athletic looking build. He was wearing a blue baseball cap and stood at least 6 inches taller than Lauren.

He reached for Tyler's leash and began:

"Please excuse Tyler, he doesn't know any better. He's not shy and is very obvious when he likes someone." At that moment, Tyler dropped the frisbee at her feet and sat beside her. He looked up with soulful eyes and patiently waited.

Pointing to the frisbee with her newly manicured hands, "Do you mind if I throw it?"

"Go ahead, Tyler would love it."

Lauren threw the frisbee into the edge of the surf and Tyler ran to retrieve it.

"Do you ride often?" Wayne pointed to the bicycle.

"Yes, I ride at least 25 miles a week, sometimes 50."

Wayne's wide smile grew, now staring into her eyes as she shyly looked away. Tyler began to gently nudge her to throw the frisbee again. She threw the bright orange disc across the empty long stretch of beach towards the dunes. Tyler ran like he had been shot out of a cannon; his long graceful body, hair flowing, moving quickly across the beach. Lauren and Wayne silently watched Tyler retrieving, then Wayne broke the silence.

"Can you believe this beach? I've never seen such a wide-open beach with so few people. Tyler and I love it! Is this your first time on Kiawah?"

"No, I used to come here when I was in high school. Obviously, been a minute..."

They both smiled.

"But, it's as beautiful as I remember. I love it here too!"

Tyler, now sitting beside Lauren, dropped the retrieved toy at her feet. With a panting smile, his big beautiful hopeful eyes looked to her to launch the disc again. She reached down and grabbed the frisbee.

"Tyler is persistent when he makes a new friend. I hope that you aren't in a hurry. Looks like he's not going to let you leave."

"Ok Tyler, Just a few more." She threw the frisbee which caught the ocean breeze and floated down the beach several hundred yards. Tyler ran at top speed; eyes fixated on the bright orange floating object and caught it in the air.

"Wow! He is so fast and graceful."

Wayne blushed like a proud father, then asks:

"You know of any Tyler friendly restaurants nearby? After being in conference meetings all day, I hate to leave him in the condo alone again tonight."

"The Salty Dog Cafe at Bohicket Marina not

only allows dogs, they're very dog friendly and have outdoor seating. They have live music most nights. It's also a great place to watch the sunset over the waterway..." Realizing that she sounded like an advertisement, she trailed off.

"Sold me on The Salty Dog. It sounds perfect! Thanks from Tyler! He loves the name of the restaurant."

Lauren realized her mistake, as she'd be at the Salty Dog with Kathleen tonight.

This guy is gonna think that I'm stalking him if I don't say anything.

"Maybe we will see you there, since I'm gonna be there with a friend tonight."

Maybe that answer was worse than stalking, more like a flirty hint to meet me there. Embarrassed again. Wow! Why am I so flushed? As she pondered, she became truthful with herself.

Because Wayne is so good looking. That's why.

Lauren did not like the vulnerability of her feelings. She grabbed the handlebars of her bike, lifted it up, and started to stroll away. Wayne, noticing her intention to leave, leaned in closer and with a friendly smile, said

"If we see you at the Salty Dog, we'll definitely say 'Hello'".

"That would be great!" Lauren turned her back to Wayne and began to jog away towards the bike path. Wayne and Tyler both stared with heads tilted and mouths open as she walked away. Both caught off guard that the conversation and frisbee throwing had come to an end so abruptly. Wayne realized that he had missed Step 2 of his 10 step plan.

That's ok. Steps 3 and 4 are now complete.

"Lauren!" Wayne called loudly over the sound of the surf. Lauren turned to face the pair.

Wayne yelled even louder:

"We really hope to see you there!" Wayne immediately thought:

Later, I have plans for you...

He could not help that he felt an instant connection to Lauren. It was crazy that Wayne's heart was palpitating at the thought that he would see this woman again in a few hours. She gave a big smile, waved goodbye and vanished with her bike over the dune. Wayne and Tyler looked at each other for a moment, then Tyler picked up the Frisbee and dropped it at Wayne's feet.

CHAPTER 17

Trapped

Once out of sight, Lauren felt panicked at the thought of running into Wayne tonight. Usually, she felt so comfortable with the laid back atmosphere of The Salty Dog and with Kathleen. She had not given any thought to what she would wear tonight. Now suddenly, she couldn't think of anything else. Pondering her outfit options, she pedaled her bicycle back to the Villa, glanced at her phone. 5:17pm. Then she did a quick internet search.

"Sunset on Kiawah Island tonight is 7:51pm." One of the unusual things about Kiawah Island is being able to see the sunrise over the Atlantic Ocean while on the eastern shore and the gorgeous sunsets over Bohicket Creek waterway on the west side of the island. Lauren would need to leave the Villa at about 7:00 to get to the restaurant and get seated in time for sunset dinner. Basically she had an hour and 43 minutes until she needed to leave. That does give her time to drive each way to the roundabout to go to the shops at Freshfields Village for a new outfit. She would only have about 20 minutes to shop, leaving 50 minutes to shower, blow dry her hair and apply makeup.

Yes. I've got time..But I'm gonna need to stay focused. Don't get distracted.

Lauren used the key that Jay gave her to enter the Villa. She immediately saw him sitting in the dining room on his laptop.

"Hey Jay." As she continued down the hallway to the guest room.

"Lauren! The security system was installed today! I'm about to go live with all of the cameras and electronic locks." Jay smiled with delight. He looked almost frantic with excitement.

"I gotta grab a quick shower and run to Freshfields Village before meeting Kathleen for dinner. Haven't heard from her, have you?"

"Yes. She's been delayed at the Atlanta airport, but she's booked on the next flight. She said to tell you that she will meet you at The Salty Dog for a sunset dinner."

"Great! Thanks JJ. Sorry, I mean Jay! Gotta hurry!"

She shut the door to the guest suite quickly to avoid becoming distracted in conversation. She then hurriedly undressed, showered and washed her hair. As she dried off, she caught a glimpse of herself in the bathroom mirror.

Not too bad for a 37 year old divorced mother of two. All the hard work is paying off. She stepped onto the digital scale: 121.

Down 38 pounds in the last year. Riding my bike every day is worth it! Next, she smoothed lotion on her legs.

I do have nice muscular legs. Definitely want to wear something like shorts tonight. Nothing dressy. Bohickett he marina is so casual. Shorts would be perfect. I'll look for those first at Freshfields. Too bad that none of my clothes fit." She pulled on her Capri pants and a boxy unisex yellow t-shirt. Noticing how nice her toes look from the pedicure today.

Sparkly flip flops too! Lauren slid her feet into her platform flip flops. Then she began to blow dry her hair. She noticed a few gray hairs mixed throughout her long curly brown hair.

How have I never noticed this before? Is it my lighting at home or have I just been in denial? Nothing I can do about it tonight. She looked through her makeup bag, pulled out the cc cream, dotted it under her eyes and used a sponge to blend it. Next, she applied mascara, lip stain, then lip gloss, and looked in the mirror.

Good enough.

Lauren looked at the time, 6:01 pm, grabbed her ID, and shoved it into the pocket of her capris. Noting the villa key that Jay had provided earlier, she placed it in her front pocket.

Car keys? Where are my car keys? Found them! Running a little behind. Gotta stay on track and can't get distracted. She opened the guest bedroom door and walked into the hallway. Jay was still staring at the laptop in the front room, glued to the screen watching something that he can't take his eyes away from. He jumped, startled and closed the laptop screen to hide it from Lauren's view.

"I'm heading out. See you later Jay."

"Lauren, Wait. First, you need to download this app and create a username and password, so I can send you a numeric code to link your phone to the Villa electronic key system. Afterwards..."

Lauren cut Jay off. "Listen, I've got to go. Can we do this later?"

"If you don't, You won't be able to get into the villa tonight." Nervously he ran his long fingers through his dark hair as he looked up over the laptop.

"How long will it take?" She was impatient to get out the door.

"Just a few minutes... Well, a few minutes after the app has downloaded... depending on your cell service carrier." Lauren inwardly groaned and looked at her phone again.

6:06 pm. If I take the time to download the app and register, I'll miss my window of opportunity to go shopping.

With pleading eyes, she looked at Jay.

"Can I leave my phone here with you while I run to Freshfields Village? Would you mind downloading the app and getting it set up for me? I would really appreciate it."

"Yes I will do it for you but you're gonna have to give me your passwords."

"Thank you Jay! Screen lock code is 1234,

What else do you need?"

"Just your email address and password."

"LWright999@gmail.com. Password is my childrens names: Justinandmargaret".

Lauren handed her lifeline to Jay and walked out of the villa. She looked at the time again, this time on the dash of her car. 6:11pm Although the weather was perfect outside, the Accord was hot inside. She started the engine, opened the sunroof, then stood outside with the door open to let the trapped hot air out.

I don't want to undo my shower by getting sweaty just before shopping and dinner.

When she turned her back to slide into her car, she heard running footsteps behind her. Lauren jumped into the car and started to shut the door. Before she could close it and without warning, Lauren felt the full weight pushing her against the car seat. Unable to move, she was trapped.

CHAPTER 18

False Accusation

Kiawah now reminded Kathleen of her long lost friend, Lauren Humphrey. Most of the time, Kathleen pushed away the hurtful memories. However, with too much time to reflect, she allowed her thoughts to wander to the last time that she had seen Lauren. *20 years*?

She now remembered how her father had looked at Lauren that night on the beach. His face transformed as his eyes became evil with big black pupils fixated on Lauren as she danced at the campfire in her crochet bikini top and denim Daisy Duke's. Kathleen had seen that look many times before and had dreaded it, but that night it had terrified her. She had feared that Lauren would fall subject to her father's cruelty and could not let the abuse happen. So she chose to intentionally sacrifice the relationship and accused Lauren of stealing cash from her handbag.

Falsely accused her...She was so devastated when her parents came early for her pick up. I felt terrible, however it was better than Dad's cruelty.

Kathleen took another long sip of her

margarita and tried to convince herself that she had done the right thing all those years ago…

CHAPTER 19

10 Step Plan

Wayne looked at his phone: 6:11 pm.

Getting close to sunset. He gathered his chair and dog leash. Tyler, now with the frisbee in his mouth, followed Wayne towards the boardwalk at public access #16.

Just a short walk to the Villa. As they exited the bike path into the parking area, Tyler lifted his nose into the air, ears perked up and straightened his tail as if he were pointing at a bird. Suddenly Tyler darted across the parking area. Wayne began to chase the dropped leash then realized that Tyler was running too fast. Wayne looked up to see Tyler disappear behind a gray older sedan. As Wayne got closer, he recognized the driver as Lauren. Tyler had half of his body in the car on top of her lap. He took up the entire space between the steering wheel and Lauren's chest, essentially pinning her to the seat.

"I'm so sorry. I can't believe he did this." Then Wayne turned towards the dog and shook his head.

"No Tyler, bad dog!" Wayne dropped the

chair and grabbed hold of Tyler's leash.

"No worries! There is no such thing as a bad dog. He's just being friendly!" Lauren reached to scratch Tyler's ears as Wayne pulled the dog out of the car.

"Are you ok? Tyler thinks he's a lapdog, but his claws can do some damage."

Lauren looked at her capris pants now dirty with sandy dog prints, her shirt wet with salt water and dog drool.

I just took a shower, now look at me! But instead answered

"I'm good! Nothing that laundry soap won't wash out."

Wayne, now standing between the car door and Lauren.

"Are you sure? I can pay for the dry cleaning or buy you new clothes!" Actually, Lauren had the bejeezus scared out of her, but she didn't want to appear frail. So she looked up making eye contact with Wayne.

"No, really, I'm fine."

He studied her for a moment as if he might say something, started to speak then stopped himself. Instead Wayne smiled at Lauren. She couldn't make herself turn away from his gaze.

"Okay, I believe you. But at least let me buy you a drink tonight. That is… unless the 'friend' you're meeting tonight is really a date." Lauren continued to feel her heart beating out of her chest from the earlier scare when Tyler pinned her.

With Wayne still between Lauren and the car door, she answered

"No… I mean Yes." Then she began to calm down from the startle and clarified, with nervous.giggle:

"Yes, you can buy me that drink. And no, it's not a date. I'm meeting my friend Kathleen."

"Great. It's settled. I will see you at the Salty Dog at sunset and buy you a drink."

Wayne closed the door of the car, walked to the sidewalk with Tyler and waved goodbye. He didn't want to give Lauren a chance to change her mind. Wayne had plans for Lauren later but he had to be patient now.

Again, Lauren looked at the car dash.

6:16pm. *Good thing I'm meeting Kathleen at the restaurant. Now I don't have time to come back to the Villa. After shopping, I'll wear my new clothes and head straight to the restaurant.* She drove out of the parking lot and onto Kiawah Island parkway towards the roundabout. Within moments of starting the drive, Lauren began to relax after her initial scare with Tyler and conversation with Wayne. She focused on a beautiful drive filled with the smell of pine trees, the smell of the marsh, and the smell of sweet flowers.

Wayne turned from waving goodbye to Lauren and thought to himself.

I knew that Tyler was a "chick magnet" but this is different.

Wayne often used Tyler to break the ice

with vulnerable women while on the road away from his wife and daughter. Wayne had a 10 step plan that worked almost every time.

1. Wayne removes his wedding band. He places it in his pocket. This act is a signal to Tyler.
2. Tyler finds a lone woman and places the frisbee at her feet. The lone woman usually looks around for a dog owner.
3. Wayne introduces Tyler and himself.
4. Wayne makes small talk while Tyler tries to play frisbee with the woman. He gets a feel for the woman's status. Single, married, traveling with friends or family or alone.
5. If single, traveling alone or vulnerable, Wayne asks for recommendations for dinner in a casual place that allows dogs.
6. Announce the place and tell her that you will be there tonight.
7. Offer to buy her a drink for her help.
8. Act like a gentleman and as if you can't take your eyes off of her.
9. Once she is feeling woozy, offer to walk her to her car or give her a ride.
10. Hopefully score sex in the parking lot. Then drive away, never to be seen again.

Vacation sex is the best! He thought to himself. But I gotta follow the rules in order to not get caught. No last names. Pay in cash. Always use a condom.

CHAPTER 20

It Takes a Village

Friday, April 14

Brooke drove to Freshfields Village and parallel parked on Main street outside of the Vineyard Vines boutique. Impatiently, she looked at her phone. Waiting for the photos from Corley.

Nothing yet.

Sitting in her car, she had a beautiful view of the many visitors to the town center of The Village. People strolling along the sidewalks with smiles on their faces. She looked out to the Village Green where people were gathering. Some groups were playing corn hole, others sitting on blankets, still others standing near a sign that read:

> Shag Night on the Village Green:
> Join Freshfields Village and
> Doin' the Charleston for our
> Spring Shag Night each
> Tuesday from 6:00pm to 8:00pm.

Although, it was a perfect place to spend an entire vacation day, the seconds felt like forever as she waited. Finally, she received a new message from Joleen, see Attachment. Brooke clicked to open the attachment for the auto registration for Lauren Humphrey Wright. It's for a 2012 Gray Honda Accord. Immediately she sent a text to Officer Dawkins, Detectives Howard and Daniels

"Search for 2012 Honda Accord. Gray. Contact me immediately when found."

Brooke received another message alert on her phone.

Perfect! It's from Corley.

She opened the attachment with the four photos. White swimsuit top, white swimsuit bottoms, white scalloped edge shorts, and bright blue polished toenails.

"Corley! You are the man!" She messaged him back.

Brooke stepped out of her car just after 5:30 pm, noting that the Vineyard Vines boutique closed at 7:00 pm. She entered the brightly lit retail store and was immediately greeted by a young lady in her mid 20s with a big smile:

"Welcome to Vineyard Vines. Is there anything that I can help you find?" Brooke noticed the name tag on the young woman.

"Katie, I'm Lead Investigator Brooke Mason. I'm investigating a suspicious death." Brooke flashed her badge at Katie.

"I have photos of some clothing that I would like for you to take a look at to see if you recognize them. Maybe someone purchased them within the last few days?"

"Doubt that I can help. We stay busy. But I will be glad to take a look." Katie motioned for Brooke to follow her.

"We can talk more privately over here." Once at the back of the store between clothing racks filled with spring colors of short shorts, Katie started to whisper:

"Did you say homicide? Not here on the island! Things like that don't happen here." Katie spoke in disbelief. Without response, Brooke turned her phone towards Katie and showed the first picture of the victim's shorts. Immediately Katie's face winced from the thought that the shorts may now be on a lifeless body.

"Suspicious Death, Didn't say homicide."

"Yes. That's our three and a half inch white scalloped Everyday Short." Brooke revealed the photo of the swimsuit top.

"Yes, that's our Sunseeker Bikini top in white." Before Katie can finish, Brooke flipped to the next photo of the swimsuit bottoms.

"Yes, that's ours too." Katie began to whisper again.

"Was it the lady that was here last night? Oh my goodness. No. Can't be. Is this related to that lady? She was so excited about going to watch the sunset. What happened?"

"What time?" Without answering, Brooke pressed for more information.

Katie started to tear up and didn't speak

for several seconds. She took a deep breath and regained her composure before she spoke:

"I remember her. She came in just before closing, last night. Her capris pants were covered in beach sand and her shirt was covered in dog slobber. She asked for help to purchase something 'cost conscious and casual cute' to wear to a sunset dinner." Brooke started to speak, as Katie shoved a ladies light pink Vineyard Vines T-shirt in front of her.

"She purchased this T-shirt too. Size small."
It wasn't recovered at the scene. This pink T-shirt may be relevant. Brooke snapped a picture of the shirt and tried to get more information.

"What time did she leave?"

"A few minutes before seven, just before closing. She walked out of the dressing room wearing her new clothes and carrying her dirty ones. She paid with cash. We walked to the front of the store. She thanked me and walked out onto the sidewalk. Then I locked the front door behind her. I didn't get her name, but I did notice her getting into an old gray car."

We have a witness of Lauren Wright getting into her car at 7:00 last night.

"Is there anything else that you can remember?"

"Oh! She also mentioned that she had gotten a mani/Pedi when she was in Freshfields Village earlier yesterday... Oh! And she bought a book called Washed Away at Indigo Bookstore. That's everything." Katie began to look impatient with the questions.

"I've got to get back to work. If you need anything else, you will need to talk to the owner of the boutique." Immediately, Katie turned and began a conversation with a customer coming out of the dressing room.

"That looks fantastic on you!" Katie walked away from Brooke towards the customer.

"You have been a big help! Thanks Katie."

"You're welcome."

Brooke exited the boutique and walked the two blocks over and one block down to the Kiawah Nail Sudio on the corner. While entering the salon she was quickly greeted by a receptionist.

"Detective Brooke Mason, I'm investigating a suspicious death. Did you have a customer yesterday with this color of nail polish?" Brooke turned her phone to face the receptionist

"We have lots of customers, ones who like their privacy, I don't know if we did or not."

"Listen, as I said, I'm investigating a suspicious death. Do you remember this customer?"

"I'm the receptionist, it's my job to remember people. I remember her. Yes, she was here yesterday. Paid with a debit card and tipped in cash."

"What was the name on the card and what time was the transaction?"

The receptionist typed into the laptop then wrote on a post it note and extended the note to Brooke.

Lauren H Wright 1:48 pm.

Brooke pressed for more information:
"Did she say anything about why she was on the island or with whom?"

"No, but I did see her walk into the cafe across the street."

Brooke thought about the timeline,
1:48 pm Lauren Wright finishes a mani/pedi
6:59 pm buys new clothes
3-5 am dead

Now, We just have to fill in the gaps. Noticing a missed call from John Dawkins, she returned his call.

"Dawkins here. Brooke, I got something for you. Lauren H. Wright never checked in or out at the registration desk, however a car pass was requested by 4228 Mariners Watch for a 2012 Gray Honda Accord. It was issued at the guard gate on April 13 and expires on April 20."

"Good work, Dawkins. Now we have an address at the Villas."

"Yeah, looking on the map, the Villa is near PA16."

"Dawkins, head over to 4228 Mariners Watch and see if you find the car in the parking lot."

"Sure thing."

The call ended.

Love it when agencies work together!

It was all that Brooke could do to stop her

impulse to sprint across the street to the Co-op Cafe because she was nearing her deadline to get to the autopsy. Within seconds of stepping into the sidewalk cafe, Brooke stepped back outside to take the call.

"Detective Mason here." Berfore she could finish the greeting, Joleen's excited voice began:

"Brooke, you are not gonna believe this! The vicitim's husband, Donald Wright invited Detective Howard into his house, said to tell you they're leaving Columbia now. Headed to the Morgue. ETA 7:16pm." Joleen ended the call.

In a whirlwind of thought, Brooke walked back into the cafe and turned the SC driver's license photo towards the young man behind the counter.

"Yes, she was here yesterday afternoon. She came in alone, ordered a turkey sandwich to eat here and two peach froze's to go. She sat at that table. The manager indicated a sidewalk table. Next thing you know, I bring out the Froze' and she is giggling with some guy." Brooke looked up shocked.

"With some guy? Did you get his name?"

"No name, some fair skinned guy, long dark hair. They immediately got up and walked away from each other laughing. As the man got into his car she said something about "12 minutes". They both laughed again."

"Car, what kind of car did he get into?"

"It was a Tesla, unusual color, cobalt blue."

Brooke made a mental note:
Fair skinned male, Long dark hair, Cobalt blue Tesla Last Seen with victim

"What time?"

"Give me a few minutes." The sandwich shop owner viewed the security camera video dated April 13 starting at 14:00 pm. He fast forwarded then finally reported.

"2:39 pm to be exact. If you want to see the video footage, you are going to have to get a search warrant. We take privacy very seriously on the islands."

Brooke didn't hesitate and came back with:

"I take death very seriously. Expect to hand that evidence over with a warrant. You have, however, been a huge help."

Brooke had a million things rushing through her head, she formed a plan.

Find the Tesla, find the man.

Brooke added to her April 13, Lauren Wright timeline:

1:48 pm finishes a mani/pedi
2:39 pm leaves Co-op Cafe
6:59 pm buys new clothes at Vineyard Vines
3-5 am dead
Now I just need to fill in the gaps!

CHAPTER 21

Autopsy

7:39 pm

Before Brooke entered the morgue, she sat in her car waiting until closer to 8:00 pm to walk into the autopsy, dreading the overwhelming smell of strong bleach, formaldehyde and death. She noted that Detective Howard's car is in the parking area next to Donald Wright's SUV.

He must not have been worried about the husband skipping out on us.

"Got him here! Good Job!" She texts to Detective Howard.

She sent a text to Detective Daniels:

"Search for 2023 cobalt blue Tesla Model S. Secure the area around the vehicle
and call me for further instructions." Daniels responded quickly "YM". Fortunately, Brooke knew that he would work effectively on the assignment.

Unable to procrastinate any longer, Brooke walked into the autopsy just before 8:00 pm.
First, the ME began with a visual inspection of the victim's body. Dr. Epps, measured and notated any tattoos, abrasions, scars, lacerations, ecchymosis,

or otherwise interesting or unique markings on the skin. She began recording:

"Identity is confirmed by dental records and next of kin, Donald Wright, for Lauren Humphrey Wright. Autopsy begins at 8:01 pm on April 14.

The soon to be ex husband did indeed make it to the morgue prior to his 8 pm deadline.

Dr. Epps continued:

"Based on body temperature, her time of death is estimated to be between 3 and 5am. General Appearance: Rigor Mortis has set in with the victim left side lying, as evidenced by blood having pooled on her left side. Her arms and legs are flexed into a fetal position."

"No lacerations are noted on her face."

"There is a 7 1/2 inch length by ¾ inch width by 1 ½ inch deep laceration at the level Cervical vertebrae C1 with noted penetration into the occipital region of the skull. Also noted brain stem lacerations due to occipital bone fragment impaction.

Multiple axis x-ray of the skull and cervical spine indicate bone fragments are present in the neural tissue of the brain stem, cerebellum and spinal cord."

Brooke noted to herself: *Her skull was cracked to the point of shattering into her brain.*

Dr. Epps moved to the middle back and continued to speak:

"T6 level laceration length 19 ¾ inch length, width ¾ inch and depth of 1 ½ inch.

Obvious thoracic spinal fractures at levels 5 & 6. Spinous and transverse processes displaced with lacerations into the spinal column."

"There are two circular 1" bruises present over the anterolateral cervical vertebrae 5 & 6."

Brooke notes: *made by fingers squeezing her neck.*

Dr. Epps: "No recent wounds noted over the chest, abdomen or pelvis. There are no defensive wounds noted on the arms or hands. In Fact, her hands look recently manicured." Dr. Epps took samples from under the victim's fingernails and passed them to the lab assistant.

Caught in the victim's fingernails, Dr. Epps removed a single long blond curly hair. She examined the victim's chest and abdomen without comment.

"Cesarean section nicely healed and faint incision measuring 5.5" noted at the pubic hair line."

"Victim has parallel bruises measuring 5" by 3" over her thighs. Along with several abrasions to the same said areas."

"Bilateral lower extremity flexor and extensor hypertrophy is present in musculature with an estimated 12% body fat." She focused on the ankles, feet and toes of the victim.

Dr. Epps was quiet again then:

"This polish is perfect with the topcoat intact. Looks like she has just had a pedicure within the last day or two."

Under the nails of the victim's toes, Dr. Epps collected fibers with tweezers and placed the fibers on the microscope slide.

Brooke noted possible evidence from the visual exam:

Long deep lacerations to the back of head and upper back.

Trauma= fracture = large force

Was she beaten with a long kinda sharp object with lots of force?

Bruising to the front of her neck. strangulation?

Placed on her left side in a fetal position within moments of her death.

Gave birth by c section. She had a child several years ago?

Bruising with abrasions over her thighs.

Very muscular legs and low body fat. Athletic build. Dancer? No, her toes are too nice. Runner? No blisters. Cycler? Maybe?

Beat with a long sharp but not thin object from behind? Then strangled and placed in a fetal position.

Next, Dr. Epps began the gynecological exam. She used voice to text to document for her examination.

"Gynecologic Exam Externally noted: labial bruising with discoloration to the internal labia." Inserting it into the vaginal opening then using a scope camera to produce live video, Dr. Epps looks at the video screen and continued:

"small tears throughout the inferior portion of the vaginal lining, indicative of penetration. The ecchymosis is scant throughout the posterior vaginal wall."

Brooke thinks:

The victim did have sexual intercourse within hours of her death. We don't know if it was consensual.

The M.E., Dr. Epps continued the exam with several vaginal swabs which look like long Q tips.

"Samples taken throughout the vaginal lining."

As Dr. Epps retrieved each sample, she handed it off to her assistant, who then smeared it onto a microscope slide and immediately placed it under the microscope. The exam room was silent for several minutes. Indicating that the Assistant had not found any signs of active or inactive sperm on the slide. Loudly, and out of nowhere, Dr. Epps' voice:

"Wait! I found something!" Everyone in the room jumped with a startle at the suddenly interrupted silence.

"Hand me micro-forceps. I want to retrieve it." The lab assistant sprang from her chair at the microscope and passed the forceps to Dr. Epps. After a few seconds, she spoke again:

"Got it!" The entire room held their breath waiting to hear what the "it" was. She held the sample at the end of the forceps under the bright light, close to the victims pubic hair.

"It's a pubic hair and it doesn't appear to match the victim's pubic hair." Dr. Epps handed the forceps to the lab assistant. Who quickly placed the hair on the slide and examined it under the microscope. Almost frantically, the lab assistant moved the slide and adjusted the magnification to focus.

"The root is intact!" She exclaimed.

Brooke thought out loud what everyone in the room was thinking.

"There's a good chance we can get DNA from the root."

As reality sets in, Brooke thought to herself

We can't wait on results from DNA testing. That could take weeks. We need to go with other evidence. Sexual penetration, yes. But, We don't know if it was consensual. No semen present. Used a condom? Found pubic hair not matching the victim. Follicle root is intact. Good chance for DNA.

Yeah, if I can get chief to sign off on the expense of the DNA testing.

Brooke asks Dr. Epps:

" What's your thoughts on the victim and the injuries?"

Dr. Epps looked at her from behind her safety glasses, facemask, hair cover and isolation gown.

"I can tell you that the base of her skull was hit at a very high force with a rather long, heavy object, with some type of corner. Something with a squared edge. The force was massive, breaking her skull and cervical vertebrae. The bone fragments sliced her brain stem, immediately leaving the victim paralyzed from the neck down and unable to use her diaphragm to breathe. The trauma across the middle of her upper back broke her ribs which punctured her lungs. Although she was paralyzed, I do believe that she was alive for several minutes after her injuries as her heart continued to beat. Within an hour of her death, she was placed on her left side. Time of death is estimated to be around 4 am on April 14. Several hours before her death, she did have some vaginal penetration. No defensive wounds, I think that it may have been consensual. A non matching hair with a follicle was obtained. We will send it to the lab for DNA testing if it's approved. We also found another non-human hair under her fingernails. Light brown dog maybe. And some fibers under her toenails. We will try to get a match on those. Otherwise, she was fit for a 37 year old, she had given birth vaginally and via c-section. She has very developed Bilateral lower extremity musculature. I'm sure that she regularly participates in some type of athletic activity, something that really uses the lower body: cycling, maybe roller skating or ice skating. She is approximately 5'-6" tall, 121 pounds, well-muscled."

She paused, looked at Brooke and said:

"I want answers as much as you do Detective Mason. Once I finish the internal exam I can tell you more. That's all that I have for now. Toxicology report will take another week, at least and the DNA from the pubic hair will take a minimum of weeks if it's approved for genetic testing."

Brooke knew from experience that she did not want to stick around for the internal exam. She would wait for the results. She left the mortuary after 11:30 pm exhausted and with more questions than answers.

Later that night, Brooke tried to fall asleep. But her brain will not allow her to drift off. Her thoughts raced:

Why didn't Lauren fight back? Why doesn't she have defensive wounds? Who wouldn't fight back if they were being beaten with a weapon, leaving long deep gashes and lacerations in the back of the head, penetrating the brain stem at the base of the skull? Why wouldn't her manicure be ruined while trying to stop the attacker? There were no stricture marks around her wrists. Why didn't she run away? And what caused the strange parallel bruises on her thighs? Finally, slumber came, and She drifted to sleep.

CHAPTER 22

Ben-a-dic Not-so-Much

Saturday, April 15

The next morning Brooke awoke to a text alert from Dr. Epps that the preliminary autopsy exam information was available, however the final results will not be available for weeks.

Cause of death:
Head injury with brain stem lesions in conjunction with Spinal cord injury level C1 resulting in sudden death.
Estimated time of death 3-5 am April 14.
Written Internal Exam
Heart within normal levels (WNL).
Lungs WNL
Liver WNL
Kidneys WNL
Stomach contents: shellfish and salad.
Toxicology Requested
Estimated last meal: 9-11 pm.

Brooke thought to herself,

Nothing unexpected. I'm gonna have to solve this mystery the good old-fashioned way, with lots of time, interviews, detective work.

She dressed in her workout clothes, and drove for the 50 min drive from Folly Beach to Kiawah. As she pulled into the Kiawah Island Beachwalker Park, she told herself to clear her brain for her morning run on the beach. Brooke looked at her watch: 6:17 am.

Plenty of time for a run before I go to Morris Tax and Accounting for a little sleuthing into Lauren H. Wright's work life.

Brooke started to jog down the nearly empty beach along the eastern shore, past the townhomes, and boardwalk accesses. The sun continued to rise across the skyline creating spectacular colors of the morning sky; each reflecting off of the ocean horizon.

Never gets old. Brooke thought as she looked across the infinite vastness of the sea. She turned back to focus on her run. Continuing to jog down the beach for several minutes more, Brooke found herself at PA16. She looked at her phone, 6:38 am. Only a 20 min jog down the beach from the public park to the privately owned beachfront near PA 16. She looked at the scene from afar and studied it with fresh morning eyes.

Anyone could have buried her under the boardwalk. And what was the weapon? Brooke wondered how it had only been 24 hours since Lauren Wright's body was found by Mr. Shealy and his dog. Suddenly, Brooke remembered that she hadn't gotten any background on Mr. Shealy.

Benedict was supposed to check this guy out

and get back to me. Wait, where is Benedict?

Brooke realized that she hadn't seen or heard anything from him since he left the beach yesterday morning with the 911 caller. A text would be easy to ask Benedict. However, she did not want to make it easy for Benedict to explain away his absence. Brooke needed a verbal explanation for his absence over the last 24 hours.

"Benedict here. What do you want?"

"An update on what you found out about the guy with the dog from yesterday morning. And where have you been?"

"Oh yeah! Wayne Shealy lives in a tiny town called Pumpkintown in The Upstate. Eleven years ago our buddy Wayne pled guilty to sexual misconduct and received 5 years probation. I'm sending his SC driver's license and registration to you now. Fella drives a nice 2023 Black on Black Toyota Highlander. Man, I would love to own a brand new anything. Allows his dog to ride in the front seat beside him."

Brooke interrupted Benedict,

"Did Mr. Shealy say anything else that he saw this morning on the beach related to the case?"

"No, but he did say something about a good looking woman playing frisbee on the beach with Tyler for at least half an hour yesterday. Wayne says that Tyler is a real chick magnet. I'm thinking about getting a dog now too. Says that he got lucky with her last night. They met up later at the Salty Dog to watch the sunset and drink." Something clicked in Brooke's brain like a light bulb going off. She remembered her conversation with Katie at the boutique.

The victim had entered the store with beach sand and dog slobber on her shirt! Could our victim, Lauren H Wright, and the beautiful beach frisbee woman be the same person? Was there a possibility that Lauren Wright and Wayne Shealy met on April 13th on the beach during the day... and met at the Salty Dog to watch the sunset, the night before she was found beneath the boardwalk in the early morning hours of April 14th? By whom other than Mr. Shealy? Benedict continued while Brooke was distracted in thought.

"After my divorce, I moved back in with my parents. I've thought about it all day. I'm going to get a dog. I can keep it in my room at my parents house while I'm at work. I should ask my Momma if I can have one first, but I just can't wait."
Brooke interrupted Benedict.

"Which Villa is Wayne Shealy and his dog renting this week?"

"4228 Mariner's watch. Why do you ask?" Brooke responded as she was entering the address into her phone.

"I have more questions for him. Can you meet me there? Don't make any contact until I am on scene. Stay in your car." Brooke looked at her phone navigation.

"Be there in 20 minutes."

"Wait!, I'm not done! I'm here. Been here

keeping watch on our Mr. Shealy. He brought the dog out to take a piss about 6:02 am then went back inside by 6:11 am. But here's the real kicker. Found the Honda at the Salty Dog Cafe last night around midnight. Roped it off and lifted a bunch of prints from the outside." Brooke protested

"You found the victim's car and didn't tell me. I had Howard and Daniel on it last night!"
In Benedict style, he continued "I knew that you needed some beauty sleep. So I told Rob and Matt about the car. Then sent all the prints from the outside to the lab. So, I suppose we need a warrant signed by a judge to open it?" Benedict finally paused long enough for Brooke to answer:

"Yes, or find the keys." Brooke retorted sarcastically.

"Hey Mason, I was gonna call you first thing this morning.
You've been busy. Want to know something? I can get it towed away."

Brooke realized that she has greatly underestimated Benedict. Not only had he identified that Mr. Shealy had a previous arrest record, Benedict had tailed him for the last 24 hours. And he found the victim's car.

"Good detective work Benedict." Brooke finally admitted out loud.

"Keep your tail on Mr. Shealy. I'm going to the Salty Dog to check out the victim's car."

CHAPTER 23

Burner Plan

Kathleen looked at her phone, as her four large suitcases and two carry-on size suitcases were being loaded into the trunk of the limo that Jay had arranged for her from the Hartsfield-Jackson Airport. She passed a $20 bill into the hand of the local who had guided her through the baggage claim, then slipped into the open back door of the limo. Taking her phone out of her handbag, Kathleen planned to freshen her makeup and text with her mother during the drive to Peachtree Plaza. She had given up on making it to Kiawah tonight and planned to shop at the Peachtree Mall before retiring to a hotel. She would take the 12:20 flight tomorrow afternoon to Charleston. At that moment her door opened and the driver offered Kathleen a burner phone.

"I was told to give you this phone once you are in the privacy of the limo. Yours is not safe to use." Kathleen took the burner phone from the driver and opened a text message:

"Kathleen, It's Jay. Things are not going as planned!"

CHAPTER 24

Latte for USB

Brooke was frustrated that she couldn't search the car without a warrant. However, she could have it towed and the tow company could allow Brooke access to inspect the contents. Which she did. Inside, Brooke did not find Lauren Wright's phone or car keys. Instead she found a USB drive in the center console and a post it note with handwritten notations:

$118,324.87
$86,593.68
Jennifer lunch

Brooke sent Joleen a text. "Good morning, are you willing to exchange a caramel latte for help with a USB drive?"

"Of course!"

Brooke went to Starbucks drive thru for Joleen's latte, drove to the police station, parked and walked inside. Entering the foyer, she couldn't miss Joleen with her big, thick, curly hair and tall stature. Dressed in her blue police uniform, Joleen quickly waddled towards Brooke as she could hardly contain herself with excitement. Leaning into Brooke's ear as she took the latte from Brooke's hand,

"We got a match on some of those prints that Benedict collected." Joleen paused dramatically, taking a big sip of the latte. Then continued, almost whispering

"There was a partial palm print found on the driver's side door of the victim's car.
Never guess who it matches?" She paused again,

"The 911 caller Wayne Shealy." Joleen revealed with great pleasure.

"So he knew Lauren Wright?" Do we know how they knew each other?"

"Things that make you say Hmmm. Small world." That's some good detective work for Benedict, Brooke pondered the new information.

Now we can place the victim and the 911 caller, Wayne Shealy, at the Honda. We just don't know when the print was placed or if they were together when it was placed.

"You have your caramel latte, here is the USB." Smiling, Joleen placed the USB drive into her desktop and opened the files.

"Looks like financial data from a place called: Morris Tax and Accounting."

"Anything jump out at you?"

"Yes, two entries are highlighted in red. One from last year $118,324.87 and one from this year: $86,593.68." Brooke looked at the post it note which contained the same dollar amounts.

"I'm going to Rivers Avenue. The husband

will be here at 9:00. Stall him. I will be back as soon as I can." Brooke scooped up her coffee, got into her car and headed West on Interstate 26 towards Rivers Avenue to Morris Tax and Accounting.

CHAPTER 25

Ancient Ides of April

Detective Brooke Mason entered and introduced herself to the receptionist. After only two minutes, was buzzed through the doorway by the receptionist and shown into the founder, Mr Morris' office after standing in the jam-packed waiting room.. Based on the number of people in the waiting room, she was pleasantly surprised at the quick response time.

As she entered the "70 era decorated office", the word ancient popped into her head as she noticed the gentleman behind the desk. He looked old, frail, yet the lines of his face looked frozen in anger as he attempted to stand, using the desk to push himself out of the chair. He forced a smile and motioned for her to enter his office. Then sat back down in his swivel chair and looked up to Brooke impatiently.

"Mr Morris, my name is officer Brooke Mason and I am investigating a suspicious death of one of your employees. Can you verify the employment of Lauren Humphrey Wright?"

"Wait did you say suspicious death? Lauren,

No, it can't be. She just started here in January. What happened?" The deep wrinkled lines in his face must carved with that angry expression. He appeared more frustrated than suprised.

"We're not sure Mr Morris. We're trying to determine her cause of death. Do you know of anyone who would want to harm Lauren Wright?"

"No, I can't think of anyone." He had answered quickly and without much thought.

He is quick with his answers. Why's he in a hurry?

"Has Lauren received any type of disciplinary action at work recently?"

"No, she has not." Again, without contemplation, he had quickly answered.

"Can you show me Lauren's employment record?"

"No, to protect our firm, access to her work performance will require a subpoena. Let's move this questioning along.. What do you need to know?"

"Do you have a current address?" Brooke was shocked by his fast recovery from the news of Lauren's death and his abrupt answers.

Is he just an angry old man, or is he hiding something?

"Yes." Now reading from the large screen: "She was living at 3643 Rivers Avenue apartment D, here in North Charleston. What else do you want to know."

"So you said that Lauren was hired in

January?"

"Yes, January 8th was her first day."

"And when was the last day that she showed up for work?" His dark eyes met Brooke's. It was apparent that the question was a sore subject. He pursed his lips then began a rant:

"April 12th! She was here on April 12th. But can you believe that she had that gall to take personal vacation time starting Thursday, April 13th.. Can you beleive that she demanded vacation days on April 14 and 15. You do realize that the week of April 15, is the busiest week of the year for an accounting firm!" The anger in his voice now matched the lines on his face.

That's why he's so angry…doesn't seem bothered by his employee's death.

"So Mr Morris, to confirm, the last time that you saw Lauren Wright was in the office on Wednesday, April 12th?"

"Yes, that's the last time I saw Lauren." Brooke now decided to change her line of questioning. She wanted to know more about the information found in Lauren's car.

"Do either of these figures mean anything to you?" Brooke showed Mr. Morris the post it note.

"No. But this is an accounting firm. Lots of numbers here." Shrugging his shoulders.

Maybe someone else is loose lipped.

"Do you mind if I ask other employees about Lauren?"

"Sure, go ahead. Nothing to hide here. Just know that this IS April 15. The busiest day of the year for our tax firm."

"I assure you, Mr. Morris, I will be efficient with my questions. May we use the conference room? It would help to keep this matter more private and speed the interview process."

Hesitantly, Mr. Morris agreed

"Yes, Be quick." He snapped.

"Thank you, good day."

Brooke exited his office and spotted the nameplate on the outside of the first cubicle to the left of Mr. Morris' door, "Jennifer Morris".

Jennifer... the same name on the post it note, found in the center console of Lauren's car? This is too good to be true!

"Miss Morris, please tell me about your relationship with Lauren Wright." Jennifer's face became distorted for a second with a look of shock. But in an instant, she calmed the fearful look and casually answered

"Yeah, we work together."

"Were the two of you close?"

"No, not really."

"Did you ever get together outside of work?

"No, we weren't that kind of friends."

"Do you know of anyone who would want to harm Lauren Wright?"

"No of course not! What's this all about?"

"Miss Morris, I'm here to investigate a possible homicide of Lauren Humphrey Wright.

"Do either of these numbers mean anything to you?"

Immediately, Jennifer Morris' face turned pale as if she may be sick at any moment.

"Jennifer Morris, we have reason to believe that you are misleading us. We have surveillance footage showing the two of you having lunch together. Here's footage of the two of you getting out of your cars talking, walking towards a taco truck, and getting into a Honda Accord. Can you confirm that this is you getting into Lauren's car?"

"Yes that is me we did have lunch that day." Jennifer began to cry, then she began to cooperate:

CHAPTER 26

Taco Truck with a Twist

Flashback
Tuesday, March 21

On the day that Jennifer and Lauren met for lunch, Lauren pulled up to the bright orange and red Rico's Taco Cafe truck at 11:52am. The location was familiar, as it's just down the street from the Morris family accounting firm and across the street from her new apartment. Noticing that Jennifer's car was not in the parking area.

Good. I'm the first one here. Lauren parked farthest away from the food truck. She gathered her thoughts and encouraged herself.

I can do this, she said to herself as she took a deep breath. She inhaled through her nose then blew out slowly through her parted lips. Trying to relax, Lauren decided to listen to some music. Dreams by the Cranberries plays on her radio.

Is this karma speaking to me?

At 12:08 p.m. Jennifer finally pulled into the parking area next to the taco truck. She parked her ruby red Miata MX-5 beside Lauren's car and stepped out of her convertible. Lauren noticed how thin and frail Jennifer appeared, like a stick figure balancing a full sized head, as she walked to Lauren's open car window and asked,

"What's this all about? Why are we meeting here at a taco truck?" Lauren opened her car door and got out to stand beside Jennifer.

"First, let's order lunch. Then we can sit in my car and I'll tell you everything."

They walked to the taco truck, which smelled absolutely fabulous to Lauren. She ordered the chicken tacos and Jennifer ordered an Asada burrito. Once the food was ready, as instructed, Jennifer walked to the passenger side of the car, opened the door and sat down. There she saw a sticky note with two amounts $118,324.87 and $86,593.68. She held the sticky note out to Lauren and said:

"Oh here! This was on your seat."

"No, that's for you."

"For me? What? Do you need to borrow money?"

"$118,324.87. It's the total amount of money that you embezzled from Morris Tax and Accounting last year." Jennifer's face quickly turned from shock to one of strained innocence. Lauren could see that Jennifer was going to deny everything. She became proactive.

"Okay, you can't BS me. I already know it's you. I already know exactly how much you've embezzled. I already know how you did it. So ditch that fake innocent face and listen to what I have to say." Lauren took a bite of her taco and began to eat as if they were having a casual conversation. After continuing to take several bites in silence, she looked over to Jennifer in the passentger seat.

"Oh that is so good. How's yours?"
Jennifer, too astonished to eat, had not even taken a bite of her burrito. She used a plastic knife and fork to cut the burrito open. Hesitantly, she took a small bite.

"Why did you ask me here? Are you going to rat me out to my family?" Jennifer asked.

"I wanted to get you away from the firm, because I have a proposition for you. Instead of telling your family about your embezzlement." Turning towards Jennifer, Lauren looked her in the eyes,

"You pay me $20,000 in cash to forget what I know about last year's embezzlement."

"What? Are you crazy? I don't have that kind of cash." Jennifer protested.
Lauren continued,

"Then, for the future blind eye, you pay me 20% at the end of each quarter."

"You must be insane! Why would I do that?" Jennifer's mouth literally dropped open.
she said "You are out of your mind.
There is no way I'm paying you $20,000 nor will I pay you 20% of every dollar I make in the future."

"That's where you're wrong," Lauren said. "I can rat you out to the family and the firm and the IRS. Or, you can partner with me and pay me to keep my mouth shut and continue on with your happy lifestyle." Jennifer's face changed to a look of pondering disbelief. She looked as if she was mulling it over. She started to speak and closed her mouth. After a long pause, Jennifer conceded to speak first:

"Let me digest all of this. Give me until tomorrow."

Lauren looked at Jennifer and said,

"I'm giving you a choice here. Pay me or come clean and lose your lifestyle. Now, get out of my car. I'll expect your answer tomorrow."

CHAPTER 27

Strand Feeding

Jennifer Flashback
Tuesday, March 21

Jennifer got out of Lauren's car and slid into her Ruby Red Miata. Driving away, still baffled at the conversation.

Oh shit, I did it this time! How in the hell am I going to get out of this one? As she drove down Rivers Avenue, Jennifer decided that she couldn't go back to the office. Her brain couldn't possibly work with all of the anxiety she was experiencing. Continuing to self talk as she merged into traffic on Interstate 526, Jen drove toward the beach.

Try not to hyperventilate, breathe, Jen. Slowly in, take a breath, hold it, blow slowly out. Feeling light headed. Another deep breath, inhale, hold it, and exhale. That's better. Jennifer continued to calm herself as she made the left turn on Main Road. She contemplated her meeting with Lauren as she entered the roundabout and exited towards Kiawah Island, turned right into Beachwalker Drive, following it along the Kiawah River to the Public Beach Park. There she looked in her gym bag for a change of clothes and shoes. Now wearing shorts, Jennifer walked down the long path to the beach. So overwhelmed in thought that she scarcely noticed that she reached the peak of the boardwalk. She paused and glanced left and right down the beach.

No one within 50 yards. Perfect.

Jennifer walked down the boardwalk and stepped onto the deep thick sand near the dunes. Her long thick blonde hair was now slapping her in the face in the wind. She creeped towards the shoreline, stopping just short of the retreating tide. Standing in the dense wet soil of the beach, Jen focused her eyes towards the infinity horizon, and looked across the Atlantic Ocean. She took a deep breath, inhaled as much of the ocean breeze as possible, then exhaled slowly as if trying to keep as much as possible in her lungs. Panic attack now over, Jennifer's head, heart and lungs are able to function at a normal rate. She glanced left and right again. Still no one was near, she began to walk along the shoreline just outside of the wet tide pools. She passed Public Access #2 and continued walking along the beach.

How did Lauren know? I really do plan to pay it back. It's just gotten outta control.

Jennifer began to analyze the situation with Lauren as she stepped around shells and sand dollars in her path.

So out of control.

She looked at the post-it note:

$118,324.87 last year and $86,593.68 in the first quarter of this year. Really? it doesn't seem like $204,000! How in the world did it get to be that much money?"

Jennifer mentally lists her "expenses" for the first quarter Jan, Feb, March in her head:

Down pmt on a condo: $40k
Travel Paris : $24k
Furniture: $13k
That's only $74k. Where is the other $12k?
Last year:
Cash for a MX-5 Miata: $43k
Travel Costa Rica: $16k
Travel Paris: $20k
Travel Cabo: $14k
That's $93k. Leaving $25k.

A jellyfish had beached itself in a tidal pool. Jen walked around the jellyfish and leaned over to inspect the blob with childlike curiosity.

No movement of the tentacles. He's a goner.

She stood up and continued to walk along the beach.

Regardless, the sum is a large amount of money.'..Honestly, more than I expected... It would be impossible to pay back that amount of money now... It would take a lifetime... Certainly would be easier to pay the $20k to Lauren, than to pay $204,000 back to the family firm. Continuing to walk along the shore, Jen said out loud,

"And a lot less disgraceful." Then began to ponder to herself again.

But where in the world will I get $20k? If I had money, I wouldn't have "borrowed" the money in the first place.

Jennifer continued to walk along the beach in deep pondering thoughts about how to get some fast cash. She looked up at the boardwalk and realized that she had walked all the way to PA12. Not wanting to be any further from her parked car, she does an about face and walks back down the beach in the direction that she came from.

Jennifer suddenly saw a dolphin break the surface of the water. Almost majestic in the quiet beauty as the dorsal fin raised from the surf then quietly resubmerged. She knew to scan the same area on the water because she had learned that dolphins are social water mammals who travel in groups called pods. Sure enough, after scanning the water for several seconds she spotted the dorsal fins of a Momma and baby dolphin side by side, as they quietly rose out of the water together then quietly disappeared. Distracted from her worries, she watched across the waters. Now counting, there were seven in the pod surfacing at different times in slightly different places along the beach then disappeared into the Atlantic. As a child she had gone on a wildlife tour with Captain Martin out of Bohicket Marina to see the unique feeding style of the Atlantic Bottlenose Dolphin. The mothers teach the baby dolphins to swim ashore in groups at low tide to strand fish on the beach. The pod then gobbles them up before using the retreating wave to unbeach themselves and slide back into the ocean.

Strand feeding,

She mumbled to herself, then began to walk quickly along the beach again and focus on her dilemma.

I wish that Lauren had never come to work at the accounting firm! Why does she think that I should split our family money with her?

As she now gazed down at the shell line, horizontal to the shore, she noticed the large black triangular object nestled amongst the broken shells.

Could it be a shark's tooth?

As a child, the Morris family often visited the beach, she developed a keen eye to spot the shape amongst the shells. Excitedly reached down and retrieved the tooth that was almost as large as her palm.

That's got to be the biggest shark's tooth that I have ever found!

She cradled the large gray and black tooth in her hand and snapped a few pictures before returning it to the beach, placing it in plain sight along the shell line for some other beach walker to find. Jennifer had been taught to return all nature to the beach and to leave the beach as she found it, shells, shark teeth and all! She stood up and snapped a photo of the tooth in its resting place before turning her thoughts back to her dilemma.

Really? What is Lauren thinking? Trying to

make it look like I'm embezzling money when really, I'm only borrowing it. Yeah she's the one that is trying to blackmail me.

What gives her the right to blackmail me? No! I'm not just going to stand by and let her take our family money! I'm not going to stand by and let her blackmail me. I'm going to do something about it.

Jen made the decision to do something to stop Lauren from stealing money from her family.

Saturday, April 15
8:32 am

Jennifer's reflection of the events of her meeting with Lauren now over. She turned her gaze to Brooke, and with tears streaming down her face:

"I did "borrow the money" but I did not hurt Lauren. I just wanted her to stop trying to blackmail me. So I confessed to my grandfather the very next day."

Brooke began:

"I will need you to come to the station to take your prints and DNA sample to rule you out as a suspect."

"Absolutely, I can come now. I want to be ruled out because I didn't do anything."

"Yes, I'm heading back to the station now. Let me follow you there.."

Brooke stood up and motioned for Jennifer Morris to do the same. Just as they were about to exit Jennifer's office, Mr. Morris walked into the room with Lauren's personnel file.

"You may want to look into Lauren's soon to be ex-husband, Donald. He is still listed as next of kin and is still the beneficiary on Lauren's $200,000 life insurance policy."

"Got it. Thank you Mr. Morris. Your grand-daughter, Jennifer, is going down to the station to help with the investigation."

"Is she under arrest?"

"No, she has just agreed to come to the station to provide her DNA and fingerprints. We want to rule her out on prints found on Lauren Wright's car."

"The minute that you walked into the office, my receptionist contacted our family attorney, Ronald Byrd. He is en route to our firm." He turned to face Jennifer.

"Jenn, baby, we got this under control. You no longer need to answer questions or go to the station. Tell Detective Mason that you request to have your attorney present for any further questions."

Jennifer Morris looked at Brooke, sat back down, placed her boney elbows on the conference table, crossed her skinny arms, and declared defiantly

"I would like to seek the counsel of my attorney."

Mr. Morris began a sermon on police officer interrogation techniques.

"No you are not taking my grand-daughter

to the police station on April 15! It's tax day! Not my grand-daughter, you will not hold her in a small room without cigarettes for hours, tell her false information, pressure her to admit to things that she never did, pretend to be helpful, I've seen CSI…"

The receptionist interrupted Morris' rant.

"Mr. Byrd is here to see you." Mr. Morris turns to Brooke

"Now, if you will excuse yourself, Jen would like to speak privately with her attorney."
Then turned to the receptionist,

"Show Detective Mason to the door please. She was just leaving."

Brooke was relieved to be excused from the office building. She needed some fresh air. Opening the exterior door of the office, Brooke felt the beautiful sunshine on her face and sneezed.

Happens every time. She thought to herself. An approaching man says:

"Bless you!"

"Thank you, Sir." He smiles, makes eye contact, nods his head, and walks into Morris' front door.

CHAPTER 28

Chase Every Lead

8:47 AM
Saturday, April 15

Brooke drove away from the interview with some really good leads. Initially, she did suspect Jennifer Morris of being involved in Lauren Wright's death. However, Brooke no longer believed that the scrawny 24 year old was a murderer. Having confessed to her family about Jennifer's company theft, she was no longer able to be blackmailed by Lauren Wright. Therefore, Jennifer no longer had a motive to harm Lauren Wright. Plus, Jennifer Morris was willing to provide her DNA and prints until her grand-father stepped into the room.

"Don't rule Jennifer Morris out. But it doesn't seem likely." Brooke whispers as she drives back East on Interstate 26 to the station. Brooke's phone alerted to multiple messages as she drove. She pulled off of the interstate and returned a call to Joleen. She answered in her twangy southern drawl:

"Hey Detective Mason, the husband, Donald

Wright is here at the station. Raising all kinda caine about staying in the interview room. Says he's got to leave. Got to get back to Columbia to take care of his children and his Momma." Joleen pauses and says: "We can't hold him here against his will without charging him, how long til you get here?" Brooke looked at her navigation app:

"On my way, seven minutes."

"Gonna use the Joleen charm to keep him here." Then ended the call.

Brooke arrived at the station and immediately entered the small interrogation room where Donald Wright was waiting:

"Hi Mr Wright I'm detective Brooke Mason. Thank you for coming down to the station so early this morning. I really appreciate your cooperation. We found multiple prints on Lauren's car and we want to rule you out. That'll narrow down our search for a suspect. Do you know anyone who might want to harm your wife?"

"No! I've said that many times since I've been here." Brooke attempted to diffuse his frustration.

"Okay well let's get your fingerprints first. Then I'll ask you a few questions and we'll send you on your way. Does that sound okay?"

"Sure, let's get it over with. I have nothing to hide." While Donald was processed for fingerprints. Brooke checked her messages.

Can't believe it, Howard found the Tesla. It was driven back to Mariners watch this morning.

He has placed it under surveillance but has not approached the driver.
Driver, James Presley Rothwell Jr, entered Villa 4232 at 8:53 am. Howard is waiting on orders to proceed.
Perfect! Brooke thought to herself.

Next message. *Looks like Benedict has obtained a search warrant for the Highlander owned by Wayne Shealy. He's conducting the search at this moment at 4228. Both addresses are located near the PA16 Boardwalk.*

She calls Detective Howard,

"Hey, good work Rob. Yeah, Don't approach him, just keep him in your sights from afar." Detective Howard gave a report:

"Yeah, followed him in from the roundabout this morning at 8:32 am then drove here and entered the villa alone."

"I want to talk to Mr. Rothwell about his relationship with Lauren Wright. I'm down here at the station with the husband. Let me know if Mr. Rothwell leaves or if anyone goes into the villa."

"Benedict is carrying out a search warrant at Villa 4228 around the corner from you on the 911 caller's black Toyota Highlander. Back each other up!"

Brooke wondered if the single key found in Lauren Wright's back pocket of her white scalloped shorts belonged to the villa door at 4228 or 4232. Next she called Benedict.

"Hey Benedict, what do you have?"

"We have a pink t-shirt in the back seat."

"Stop! Is it a Vineyard Vines shirt?"

"Yeah, how did you know?"

"Lauren Wright bought four clothing items from Vineyard Vines on the evening of Thursday, April 13. She was found wearing 3 of those items. However, the pink t-shirt that she purchased was never found. What else have you found?"

"Lots of Dog hair samples, I bet that it matches the ones found on the boardwalk body. Can you believe that?"

"Find Anything else?"

"Yeah, several long brown hairs and a stain on the shirt and the back seat. Bagged em for evidence.

Probably long brown hairs belong to Lauren Wright. We have Wayne Shealy's palm prints on Lauren Wright's car. Lauren's hair and shirt inside his Highlander

"Keep up the good work. I'm going to interview the husband here at the station. We are getting his prints now. Then I'm heading to Kiawah. Howard is tailing the guy in the Tesla from the Co-op."

"Who? What Tesla?

"Keep focused on your search. But, listen out for Howard. He's only four doors down at 4232 Mariner's Watch. Back him up if he needs it."

Lastly she read a message from Joleen. The video surveillance from the Co-op Cafe has been made available without a warrant.

Good! Let's have a look.

Brooke started the video: She sees Lauren Wright enter the shop, order food, then sit outside. She is joined by a brown haired James Rothwell, they hug, they talk, they laugh, they leave at 2:39pm.
Nothing suspicious.

Brooke turns her attention back to the task at hand. She enters the interview room.

"Mr. Wright, thank you again for your cooperation. Just a few more questions before you leave. Where were you on the night of Thursday, April 13th and early morning hours of Friday, April the 14th."

"You're crazy if you suspect me.

"Really?"

"Yeah I have no motive. I was in Columbia with my children and my mother. I watched Jeopardy and hung out with my kids that night. They can all vouch for me."

"What about the $200,000 life insurance policy? What about the fact that your mother's house is in foreclosure. What about the fact that your payment on your Durango is 3 months past due. Are those good enough motives to murder your wife?" Brooke pushed.

"I can't believe that I have cooperated, and you're accusing me of murder. I'm not staying any longer. I am not under arrest. I am leaving." Mr. Wright got up and walked out the room, down the hallway past Joleen and out the front door of the station.

Brooke realized there are so many people of interest that she will need to prioritize her time. She decided to plan her next move by listing people of interest and their motives.

Wayne Shealy motive: sexual assault. Last seen with the victim at the Salty Dog hours before her death.

Donald Wright soon to be ex husband, motive: money, policy holder of her $200,000 life insurance policy.

Jennifer Morris motive: removed.

Who was this Tesla guy at the Coop James Presley Rothwell Jr.?

CHAPTER 29

Sunset with a Flash

As Brooke entered the roundabout, she decided to make a quick detour to the Salty Dog to see if there is any surveillance footage of Wayne Shealy and Lauren Wright on the night of her death. She pulled into the Salty Dog and parked in the large lot, then began to walk up the very high wooden stairs that had recently been replaced.

The edges of those deck boards are so sharp. It would leave a mark if you fell downstairs. Or kill you if you hit your head. She grabbed the hand rail and was greeted by the manager.

"Good Morning! Can I help you?"

"Hi I'm Detective Brooke Mason with the Charleston County homicide unit. I'm investigating a death that occurred on the island. I'm requesting businesses to reveal their surveillance footage. Do you mind if I take a look at the CCTV footage from April 13th?"

"Hey, come on in. No worries. I'll get you set up in my office. You can view to your heart's content. I'm preparing for lunch - sorry I can't help right now."

Although there were eight video leads and camera angles on The Salty Dog, only three are of interest to Brooke.

Once I have a timestamp on one…

I can view the same time stamp from different camera angles.

Brooke finds the footage and watches beginning at 7:45 pm from multiple angles:

Jay Rothwell, Jr
Flashback April 13

Jay pulled up to the Salty Dog and noticed the time:

7:45 pm. Just enough time to walk up to Lauren's table, watch the sunset together, then tell her how I feel about her.

He got out of the 2023 Model S Tesla, placed Lauren's phone in his pocket, and walked to the edge of the outside seating deck. The setting sun was spectacular over the creek momentarily distracting his mission. Suddenly, he heard a familiar laugh. Jay looked around the deck and spotted Lauren sitting with a handsome man, deep in conversation, laughing while sipping on a frozen drink. Jay stopped and backed up into the bar area not to be seen. He watched the conversation from afar. The man at the table with Lauren had a big golden yellow dog sitting at his feet, neither looking as if they were leaving anytime soon. Jay's heart sank.

How could this happen? I've been planning this… Where did this guy come from?

Jay sat at the bar and ordered a drink, still fixating on Lauren and the stranger. He saw Lauren reach down to pet the dog frequently. He saw the stranger continuously smile as he reached to touch Lauren's arm.

Lauren just could no longer contain her excitement when the singer with the guitar began to play: "Green Flash at Sunset" by Jimmy Buffett. She stood up from the white deck chair and began to rock side to side, swaying to the beat of the music while singing. Lauren sang the short obscure Buffet sunset song so many times as a child with Kathleen. To them it signified the end of the night of fun. A time to leave the beach and to walk back to the Villa to go to bed. While JJ and the adults continued to sit around the beach campfire.

Someone judges Lauren:

Look at her, using her body to keep everyone's attention. Look at how she's dressed, short shorts and a swimsuit top in public. Dancing provocatively like that for everyone to see. Inviting others to stare at her body. How could she feel comfortable being the center of attention while so scantily dressed? The pit of pain develops in my stomach as I remember her dancing on the beach all those years ago. Distracting the tourist while I slipped away to steal treasures and bury them underneath the boardwalk to enjoy later.

Lauren continued to sway to the beat as she sang the last verse. The song ended and she stood almost in allegiance toward the setting sun over Bohicket Creek. The sunset over the almost still water was beyond words. In awe of the bright sun creating cottoncandy colors across the sky and reflecting them back on the water. Slowly disappearing beyond the water horizon. Turning into colorful reflections in the atmosphere lasting for several minutes.

Jay became enraged:

This is my night.

Lauren turned back to the deck table, embarrassment washed over her as she realized that she had just sung the song in front of a crowd of nameless people, plus Wayne and Tyler.

Jay watched from the darkness of the bar unseen, as Lauren and Wayne ordered dinner. They ate, talked, laughed, flirted, then ordered more drinks. Jay became angrier over the course of the evening, his thoughts became spinning loops of frustration, disappointment, anger, and jealousy.

At 8:41 pm. Wayne stood up and offered his hand to Lauren. He pulled her from her chair and placed his arm around her waist. She leaned into his chest to maintain her balance. Obviously, Lauren had had too many drinks and required assistance to leave the restaurant. Wayne thought to himself.

Steps 5 and 6 complete!

Disgusted and angry, Jay left the restaurant still in the possession of Lauren's phone.

Wayne asked:

"Hey Lauren? Do you want me to use your

phone to call someone?" She unable to coherently speak at this point.

All the better, Wayne mumbles to himself.

"Do you want me to drive you?"

As they approached Wayne's 2023 Toyota Highlander, Lauren shook her head "yes" and fell unconscious. Wayne lifted Lauren into the back seat and placed Tyler in the front passenger seat. Wayne gets into the back seat.

CHAPTER 30

Step 9 Here We Come

Meanwhile, Jay drove out of the parking lot and turned left onto Kiawah Island Parkway, mumbling to himself:

Defeated by some stranger...Why does she not even consider me? It's as if I don't even exist... I've wanted to be an important part of Laurens life.

Jay passed through the guard gate with his scanner code on his driver door at 9:08 pm. The band, Cake, is playing from his playlist: Friend is a Four Letter Word. Jay increased the volume to cover his sobs. The lyrics were fitting for how Jay felt at the moment. He continued to the Villa, parked the Tesla and entered the front door using his phone. He pulled Lauren's phone out of his pocket and thought:

Her key doesn't work and I have her phone. Jay smirked, *She is going to have to bang on the door to get in here. Meanwhile, I can watch her from the cameras on my laptop. Just like I did earlier while she was in the guest suite.*

Grinning while remembering seeing

Lauren's nakedness for the first time in almost two decades. Suddenly, Jay had the most horrible thought.

What if she doesn't come back tonight? What if she spends the night with that stranger."
He becomes enraged at the thought of the stranger holding Lauren.

Meanwhile, back at Wayne's Highlander...

After having sex with the unconscious Lauren, Wayne picked her up, used her keys to unlock the car, and placed her in the front driver seat of her sedan.
And slowly drove away, the Wayne and Tyler ten step plan completed!

Hours later at the Villa...

Jay became worried about Lauren and decided to return to the Salty Dog to look for her.
Jay drove through the roundabout and exited toward the Salty Dog Cafe. He worried that he had missed his opportunity to tell Lauren that he loved her quirkiness and the snort when she couldn't stop laughing. She called it having "My giggle box turned over". Jay had never heard the saying before he met Lauren. His family was so serious. Formal people who happen to be related by birth or marriage. They never giggled.

Jay reflected on the first time that he heard Lauren belly laugh. He was 16 years old. Kathleen had begged our parents to allow Lauren to join us in Kiawah for the week. Kathleen and Lauren met at summer cycling camp. Reluctantly our parents agreed. On the first night, we were all on the beach sitting around the campfire. Momma, Daddy, Kathleen, Lauren, myself, and several out of towners that my mother was trying to impress. As Lauren started to giggle uncontrollably, then began to laugh loudly, next she began to snort, her laughter continued. The more that Kathleen attempted to quiet Lauren, the more she laughed. The look on my parents' face when Lauren told them that she couldn't help herself because her "giggle box was turned over." Jay smiled at the memory despite being anxious about Lauren.

As Jay pulled into the parking lot again at 1:03 am. He immediately spotted Lauren's gray car in the parking lot. He parked beside her car and saw her slumped at the steering wheel. His heart pounded.

I hope that she's ok.

He rushed to her car door and opened it. Although the dome light shone, Lauren did not move. Panic set in for Jay as he reached forward to touch Laurens shoulder. She was warm, he could feel her chest moving.

"Lauren, wake up! Lauren, it's Jay!" Lauren slowly opened her eyes. She recognized his face. She smiled

"Hey JJ! What are you doing here?"

"Looking for you! I was worried! Why are you sleeping in your car? Are you ok?"

"Actually, I'm not feeling very well. I'm

feeling sick on my stomach and I have a splitting headache."

"Can I drive you back to the Villa?"

"Oh Thank you! Jay, that would be wonderful!"

CHAPTER 31

Confession Under Moonlight

Watching the Salty Dog surveillance video: At 13:03, Brooke saw James Rothwell return to the Salty dog in the Tesla. Place Lauren Wright in the front passenger seat of his Tesla and drive away.

So Wayne Shealy wasn't the last person to see our victim at the Salty Dog Cafe.

Brooke forwarded the security footage to Joleen then quickly got into her car. She sent a text to Detectives Howard and Benedict.

OMW

ETA 12 min.

She turned left towards the roundabout and thought to herself,

This is going to be the longest dozen minutes of my life!

She exited the roundabout towards Mariner's watch villa 4232 Kiawah Island.

We have got to interview James Rothwell. He was the last person to see her alive. Placing him with the victim at 1:03 am. And a time of death estimated from 3-5am. So what happened between 1-3am on April 13? Who's villa does the key belong to?

Once Brooke arrived at the Mariner's Watch parking area, she stepped out of her car, and grabbed her copy of the key found in Lauren's pocket. Seeing Det Rob Howard's car, she motioned for him to join her in the parking area. Brooke whispers as she holds up the key

"I bet that this key fits villa 4232. I'm ready to meet James Pressley Rothwell, Jr."

Brooke motioned towards the Villa.

"Rob, you cover the back while I knock on the front door."

Detective Howard nodded in understanding and pulled his weapon, as he walked to the back of the villa. Brooke slowly ascended the steps to the front door, looking up, down, left and right. She wanted to be very aware of her surroundings. Looking down, she noticed stains and bits of matter stuck on the stair steps.

What is this? Dried bits of something. It looks like we need to luminol these stairs.

As she opened the screened door to the villa, she noticed that the door knob was newly replaced with a keyless entry pad.

Well the key definitely does not open this villa. Dang!

Brooke knocked on the brown wooden door and listened for some sound from inside the villa. While waiting for James Rothwell to open the villa door, She continued to scan her surroundings and noticed a security camera mounted on the corner of the villa.

I bet that video footage would be helpful.

A tall thin brown haired man with very fair skin peered from behind the partially open door.

"May I help you?"

"I'm Detective Brooke Mason with the Charleston County Police Department. We are asking for everyone's help to solve a suspicious death on the Island. Would you allow us to review your security footage? Mr…?

Brooke paused and held out her hand to Mr. Rothwell

"Jay Rothwel." He said as he opened the door wider, revealing his entire body, then extended his right hand to shake Brooke's hand.

James provided surveillance footage and Brooke watched the time stamp Friday, April 14 at 1:31am: Jay and Lauren arrive at the Villa in his cobalt blue Tesla. After parking, Jay walks to the passenger side of the car and opens the door. He assists Lauren out of the car and up the wooden stairs, with his arm around Lauren to keep her from falling. They enter the villa together.

Not on camera:
Jay helped Lauren into the bed and climbed onto the bed beside Lauren, he spooned next to her, holding her closely with his head on her rising and falling chest. Her skin feels so smooth. He has longed to feel her body against his. It's the best feeling ever to be with her. This is his lifelong dream. All coming true at this moment.

He cherishes this time together for about two hours. Then, Lauren begins to move in her sleep. She wakes up, with a stretch, and yawns. Jay snuggles in and places his arm around her to give a little squeeze. Lauren opens her eyes and begins to scream. Jay jumps back and says

"Wait, it's just me."

"Jay, What the fuck are you doing in my bed?"

She looked into his eyes and she screamed even louder.

"Get the hell out of here." She jumped up from the bed and ran toward the door but she was unable to get the door open. He walked up behind her and placed his hand over her mouth.

Jay cannot take the rejection. No, he cannot take the noise of her screams. He holds his hand tighter against her face. He says

"Lauren, Listen, I don't want to hurt you. I just want to talk."

He removes his hand and says,

"I'll be in the living room waiting. When you're ready, we can talk."

Jay opened the door with the security app on his phone and walked to the living room and sat on the couch.

Lauren thinks to herself

"What the heck just happened? Don't know, but I'm not stickin around to find out.

Still wearing her bikini top and bottom with shorts, she quickly packed all of her things into her suitcase and garment bag. Then slid on her flip flops. Intending to leave the villa immediately, she walked out of the bedroom down the hall to the landing at the top of the stairs. Jay was standing at the top of the landing. Between Lauren and the stairs. Jay said:

"We have to talk, I have things I have to tell you."

She ignored his statement and said

"I'm getting the hell out of here. Give me my phone."

Jay stared at Lauren in disbelief. And thinks: *How did this turn so sour so fast?*

"Where is my phone? Do you have my phone?"

Jay pulls it out of his pocket.

"I still have your phone."

"Give it to me now."

The pair come into camera view at 4:16 am on the front deck of the villa.

Lauren lunges for the phone, just as Jay steps to the side. Her platform sparkly flip flop catches in the deck, she jerks her head back, overcompensates and flips backwards onto the stairs. Jay could hear the flesh separate and the bones break as she flipped backwards, head first, onto the stairs then she slid down to the bottom of the steps. She remained motionless. Rushing to the bottom of the stairs, he could see that Lauren's eyes were open and she was bleeding profusely from the base of her skull. He attempted to apply pressure to stop the bleeding, but he realized that Lauren's skull was shattered and the back of her head was soft, blood continued to pour.

Quickly, Jay felt for a pulse on each side of her neck. Pressing hard on her carotid artery.

Yes! She has a very strong heart beat! But she's not breathing. And she's losing blood so fast! Just pouring out of her.

Jay looks into her eyes and sees life still there. He holds her face and looks into her eyes and says

"Lauren, I love you."

Jay began to give Lauren mouth to mouth, as he breathed into her mouth with her nose pinched, he could hear the air escaping through the pierced lungs and many fractured ribs. Unable to get her chest to fill with air, Jay checked for a pulse, felt the carotid artery in her neck again, realizing Laurens heart rate was bounding, that she was still not breathing. Jay began to realize that Lauren was not going to survive the fall. He remembered reading that a person's hearing is the last of the 5 senses to stop processing information after a person passes away.

Lauren would want to hear the ocean surf one more time.

Jay was unable to lift Lauren without support due to the broken state of her body. Trying to solve the problem quickly, he used the blue beach towel to cradle her body as he gently lifted Lauren and cradled her body. As Jay carried her, he continued to talk to Lauren then disappeared from the camera angle.

Jay recounted the events while he was outside of the camera's view to Brooke. I kept talking to Lauren. I knew that she could hear me.

Flashback:

"I'm taking you to the beach. I know that you can still hear me." Jay topped the boardwalk and carried her across the sand to the base of the dunes.

"Let's sit on the beach and listen to the ocean." He cradled Lauren in his arms and whispered into her ear. He revealed secrets that only she needed to know. Secrets, whose confessions would be drowned out by the crashing waves and would be erased by the rising tide. Jay began to confess

"I've loved you since we were children. I love your spunk. I love your laugh. Lauren, you are a beautiful person". He wrapped a beach towel around her, holding her tightly and listening to the waves crash against the shore in the stillness of the night.

Jay continued to confess:

"I'm the one that placed the flowers and the note on your chair in your office. I wanted to find a way to get you to the Villa. I needed resolution…

I attended your wedding reception, Watched you raise your children through social media… Even called your office once."

"Remember when you and Kathleen would dance on the beach to distract the vacationers? You would have them so captivated around the campfire? Well, I used to take the opportunity to steal personal Mementos from the hotel rooms. I would bury the treasures in the dunes and then come back later to have them all to myself. I have felt guilty for it my entire life! I took advantage of you, Kathleen, and the tourist. This cloud of guilt has followed me. Every day I have felt guilty about something that happened so long ago. I never felt worthy of you, Lauren. But I have always loved you."

He whispered to her in the roar of the crashing waves. His confession felt liberating, like it washed the teenage sin away from Jay's long burdened soul. He sat quietly holding her on the beach. Slowly, Jay felt the warmth leave Lauren's body.

Jay heard a dog barking and someone coming out of a villa. He pulled Lauren's body under the boardwalk and out of sight. Continuing to hold Lauren, Jay didn't want to explain what he was doing with a body under the boardwalk. He only wanted to allow her to pass away peacefully in his arms while hearing the sound of the crashing waves. He had needed to confess to Lauren. Jay hadn't thought about what he would do after he held her on the beach. Again, he heard the dog bark and pounce towards the bike trail.

Someone was coming down the bike trail. I've

got to hide.

Jay continued to lay with Lauren under the boardwalk wanting to keep her for himself. He dug a hole in the sand to cradle Laurens body, and placed her in a fetal position. She looked peaceful. He gently pushed her hair aside, kissed her beautiful face and covered her with a blue beach towel. Hearing the dog run over the boardwalk, Jay panicked. He sat still as possible while a curly haired man walked along the boardwalk overhead carrying a beach chair. Continuing to hold his breath, Jay was undetected by the dog or the owner. The man exited the boardwalk onto the beach at PA 16 and walked down the beach a little and began to set up his beach chair. Jay used beach sand at the base of the dune to hold the beach towel down in the breeze and to cover Lauren. When he heard the man's alarm go off on his phone, Jay crept from under the boardwalk and quietly walked towards PA15. As Jay made it to the end of the boardwalk, he freaked out as he witnessed a golden retriever, barking and digging at the base of the boardwalk at PA16, the man running to the dunes with his phone flashlight. Jay stopped in the shadows of the palms and did not make a sound. He saw the golden retriever and owner walk away as he made a phone call to 911. Not knowing what to do or say, Jay walked into his villa and collapsed in despair.

Present
Interview with

Jay Rothwell Jr.

"I just walked into the villa and immediately began to sob. I just could not process everything that had just happened."

"What in the world were you thinking when you didn't call 911?" Brooke could not understand.

"I was thinking that Lauren was not going to recover from this fall and she would rather spend her last few moments on the beach listening to the peaceful crash of the waves instead of the sirens and commotion."

"Then why did you cover and bury her under the dune?"

"I panicked. I wasn't ready to share her with anyone. I wanted her to have peace for a little while longer. I had planned to call 911, but I wanted her all to myself first. I was interrupted and didn't want to explain. I still can't believe that she's gone."

CHAPTER 32

Close the Loops

Jay was able to provide video evidence of the events of Lauren's fall, him rushing to her side. Holding her telling her that he loves her. Cradling her then returning later, just after 6 am without Lauren. He was sobbing as he walked back into the villa. Brooke cried as she watched the villa's security footage of Lauren's fall down the stairs. Obviously, an accident was caused by a sparkly platform flip flop on a wooden stair step, causing a severe traumatic brain injury, resulting in death.
Driving away from Mariners Watch towards the roundabout Brooke was speechless.

This case appeared to be a violent murder. However, things are not always as they first appear. Mental note to self. Always look for the objective truth, trust the facts, not emotions or speculation. No matter the source.

Kathleen Rothwell decided to do some shopping at Peachtree Mall and missed her flight from Atlanta to Charleston. Her limo finally arrived at the villa 21 minutes after Brooke pulled away in her car. Kathleen was totally clueless that

Jay invited Lauren to the Villa with the flowers and mystery note three weeks earlier.

James Presley Rothwell Jr. aka Jay aka JJ plead guilty to concealment of a corpse and was sentenced to one year house arrest, five years probation and fined $4,000. His ankle monitor was never activated.

Donald Wright collected Lauren's life insurance policy for $200,000 for her accidental death and received full custody of Justin and Margaret. They continue, to this day, to live with his mother, Marilyn Wright in Columbia, SC.

Jennifer Morris was forgiven by her family for "borrowing from the family accounting firm". She agreed to a monthly payment plan. Mr. Morris, her grand-father, added the attorney's fees to her principle, doubled the amount, and charges compounded interest monthly.

Wayne Shealy spent several days being harassed by Detective Benedict. On April 15, he was released, against his will, to the custody of his wife and daughter. They continue to be silent characters.Tyler remains loyal and has failed to speak publicly about his time on Kiawah Island.

Links to Boardwalks and Flipflops Locations

Madrid, Spain
https://en.wikipedia.org/wiki/Madrid

Toni&Guy Salon
https://toniandguy.com/salon/madrid

Toma Cafe
https://toma.cafe/en

Kiawah Island
https://www.kiawahisland.org/

Freshfields Village
https://freshfieldsvillage.com/

Indigo Books
https://www.indigobooksfreshfields.com/

Vineyard Vines Kiawah
https://www.vineyardvines.com/storedetails?StoreID=130

Co-op Cafe
https://www.thecoopsi.com/location/kiawah-island/

Kiawah Island Golf Resort

https://www.kiawahresort.com

Bohicket Marina and Market
https://bohicket.com/

Salty Dog Seabrook
https://bohicket.saltydog.com/cafe/

The Roundabout
900 Kiawah Island Pkwy

Beachwalker Park
https://www.ccprc.com/1411/Kiawah-Beachwalker-Park

WANT MORE?

Look for the next novella in The Tidal Dective Series set in Folly Beach, SC where Detective Brooke Mason investigates the suspicious death of a local surfer.

ABOUT THE AUTHOR

Vanna Byrd

Vanna Byrd spent her youth in rural Red Bank Creek, SC and earned her Master's Degree from the Medical University of South Carolina in Charleston. She and her husband of over 20 years love to explore the coast, sample craft beer, dance to live music and spend time with thier daughter.

Made in the USA
Middletown, DE
06 April 2024